PARTY HEADQUARTERS

D0835250

PARTY HEADQUARTERS

GEORGI TENEV

OPEN LETTER
LITERARY TRANSLATIONS FROM THE UNIVERSITY OF ROCHESTER

TRANSLATED FROM THE BULGARIAN BY ANGELA RODEL

Library of Congress Cataloging-in-Publication Data:

Tenev, Georgi.
  [Partien dom. English]
  Party headquarters / by Georgi Tenev ; translated from the Bulgarian
by Angela Rodel. — First edition.
    pages cm
  ISBN 978-1-940953-26-7 (paperback) — ISBN 1-940953-26-X (paperback)
  I. Rodel, Angela, translator. II. Title.
  PG1038.3.E52P37 2006
  891.8'134—dc23
                              2015027555

*This book is published within the Elizabeth Kostova Foundation's program
for Support of Contemporary Bulgarian Writers and in collaboration
with the America for Bulgaria Foundation.*

Elizabeth Kostova
FOUNDATION for
CREATIVE WRITING

AMERICA FOR BULGARIA
F O U N D A T I O N
Фондация Америка за България

Printed on acid-free paper in the United States of America.

Text set in Janson, an old-style serif typeface named for Dutch punch-cutter
and printer Anton Janson (1620–1687).

Design by N. J. Furl

Open Letter is the University of Rochester's nonprofit, literary translation press:
Lattimore Hall 411, Box 270082, Rochester, NY 14627

www.openletterbooks.org

PARTY HEADQUARTERS

1

★
HIS DAUGHTER

THE strangest part is when I see she's starting to cry. With us, tears often lead to unexpected consequences.

Even without the tears I still want to hit her, painfully hard. But when she cries it just gets out of control. The victim's magnetic attraction inflames the perpetrator. I'm driven to tears myself—out of frustration that I can't force myself to finish it off, to do absolutely everything I want to her. In exactly the order I would like.

If anyone were to see us at this moment, bawling, locked in this torture chamber at opposite ends of the bed—in the middle the bloody sheets are stained with wet spots, but not from blood, lymph, vaginal secretions, sperm, or who knows what else—could it be that some other beings are copulating here with us?—at that moment the shocked outside observer would think we are crying for each other, for ourselves.

Wrong. An incorrect judgment, a faulty interpretation of ambiguous facts. I'm not sorry. What can I say? Regret is most certainly far beyond the boundaries within which I would torment her. Tears are just one more weapon in this battle, nothing more. I must be very careful now; tears, like all water, temper freshly forged metal. Her blue zirconium glare blazes out twice as pliant, resilient, like eyes on a rifle sight, eyes like bullet tips—and I'm the bull's-eye.

On the very first day, or afternoon, rather, when we met, on that fatally happy day of our acquaintance, she explained to me that she didn't have a father. She stubbornly insisted that her father did not exist. He was alive, you see, but as soon as she spoke his name and sharply declared, *It's as if I don't have a father*—then I understood, it was all clear.

His name is K-shev.

I never imagined that I would get mixed up with the daughter of one of them. But fatal meetings are always marked by signs from the very beginning. I'm talking about fleeting clues. But no one tells you "Watch out!", you don't hear any voice yelling "Stop!" And the fact that at that very moment the angels fall silent most likely means they're egging you on. That the meeting is divinely inspired; the meeting is the beginning of the collision of love.

>>>

So his name is K-shev.

Everyone remembers their names, they're strange. And they get that way because of the people they belong to, and not the other way around. Yet it somehow seems like fate also chooses them by the sounds of their names.

Who is this person, completely anonymous behind his name? Later I began to understand, things started to become clear. But by then it was too late to save myself, I was already caught in the trap. So why bother trying to go back now to fix things? There's no point. I can only return as an observer, as remote and nonchalant as if I'm watching a stranger and not myself.

>>>

You are the reason words exist—I want to pause on this thought. That is, I want to pause precisely here to make this absolutely clear. It's doubtful I'll succeed in getting any relief or satisfaction, as much as I would like to. Perhaps I suspect there is some higher purpose or calling in pornography, when you watch and somebody shows you everything.

The moment I took my eyes from the screen, the last thing lingering in my pupils was the image of naked bodies. Everything about it screams scam, despite the originality of the moans and the excitement in the voice of the nude, sweat-drenched woman. It's a scam because of the presumed viewer, because of my gaze. This is also the source of the shame.

I leave the colorful barn, its booths with their blue doors and neon lights. The dark room and the screen overhead reflected in the mirror. Next to the armchair are buttons to select the channel, a box of Kleenex, a wastebasket with a plastic liner. The silver slit that swallows coins, black speakers that spit out sound.

>>>

I go outside. It would be frightening if it weren't night. But now there's no light, just electric sparks from the street. I light a cigarette to dull the arousal. I don't want it to stay with me, I have to separate it from myself, from my body. If I had come inside like I wanted to, I most likely would've failed all the same. But I didn't make the move, I froze up, I couldn't do it. A naked woman—pretty, by the way. And another one, looking very much the same. Both with nice, full breasts, one with long fake fingernails, the other with girlish, almost infantile fingers, both with navel rings. I shouldn't feel bad about it, yet there was some kind of anxious beauty in that shot of frantically jumping bodies. That's exactly what should've relaxed me—the precision and obvious professionalism of the action. Even to the point of seeming to give them pleasure—paid for in advance by me or someone like me. These two golden-skinned bodies impatiently jostling on top of each another, with no man in between, of course—because I wouldn't be able to stand anyone else besides myself here.

I got up and left before the final minutes, leaving behind a part of myself, my hotly beating pulse—I didn't run, but somehow, despite the tension, casually and masterfully made my way to the exit. With the professional gait of a smoker waiting for intermission to give himself over to an older and more acceptable vice, one that can be shared on the street.

\>>>

Although it's difficult for me to admit, I don't think there's anyone here who could help me. Yet I still have faith in words—they're the only thing I have left. I worship them fervently. For their sake I put up with all of you, whom I honestly couldn't care less about. You're just some mute imaginary listeners to talk at. You are the reason words exist, because otherwise it would simply be too difficult. And at least you know *who he is*.

The name K-shev scared me, took me aback. Yet the girl's flight, her shame, her self-disgust—I thought to myself in the first instant—isn't it all very unusual? It made me feel compassion for her. But also a sort of suspicion. Fear.

I've tried to make sense of it before: the thrill of suspicion is the hidden urge that incites you to crush her with your hands, with your whole body. To force her to scream, to make her cry. To hurt her, to see the real depths, the entire essence. To my regret, I was soon forced to realize that she had told me the truth. She had wanted to escape from the nightmare, but it's not as easy as simply crossing out your father's name and taking a new one in its place.

This is most likely why the angel stayed silent: he caught a whiff of compassion. But what angels, what am I even talking about—the truth is always repulsive. Since it is still too early for the truth, let's console ourselves just a bit longer on the brink of our first meeting, that moment *back then*.

Perhaps times were different then. I even suspect that they illuminated that which lay ahead, the future, with a shadowless light. Sometimes when I reminisce about a kind of *coupling*, for example, I'm trying to get at that accumulation of concentrated tenderness. Is it possible that she was perfect, despite her last name? Was it the same with my naïvety—temporarily wonderful, but naïvety all the same. When falling in love we are children, if only for a short while. *In general* we are children only for a short while, like a brief attack of perfection and light. But enough of that.

>>>

I had this dream—of something like a Communist party headquarters in a provincial town. Or in the capital, but in some rundown neighborhood. Outside the summer heat is stifling. Deathly calm, a park bathed in scorching light that bleaches the green from the trees. The immaculate walkways with whitewashed curbs, all deserted. As usual the bureaucrats are using their work time for something else. Inside the hallways are cool and it would be almost pleasant if it weren't so cold. Although there aren't any mummies here, the door-lined tunnels make it feel like some kind of space for preservation, a mausoleum. But never mind all that, what's important is the content.

The girl is wearing a Pioneer's uniform, the Communist Youth League. We're holding hands. We walk along, go up the stairs, turn down one of the hallways, I think it's the fourth floor, the top one. The sense that we are alone grows even stronger here. And again that same coolness, but when we pass through the small foyer beyond the stairs and head toward the long straight line of darkness—somewhere there the windows behind the false balustrade breathe heat on us through the glass, because of the lights outside.

She is dressed in a Pioneers uniform, like I said: a white blouse, a blue pleated skirt, if that's what they call those overlapping accordion folds. Her white socks are pulled up a little over her ankles or below the knee—that's the one thing I'm not quite sure about. Her shoes have no laces, the blue tongues are sticking straight up. Her shoulder-length hair is straight, and she wears it in pigtails behind her ears. But she isn't wearing the little barrettes that usually keep her bangs out of her eyes. Under her blouse she's wearing a tank top, cut low under the arms—we all wore those back then, even the girls. All around, like I said, there's lots of stone, granite, marble, and from time to time the wine stain of the curtains, red pedestals without statues, only here and there peeling names and letters in the flaking gold cellophane used to inscribe mottos. This is a mysterious space I have yet to dive into, at once hollow, empty, yet full of sharp edges—the building itself feels heavy. It is made up of intersecting squares and rectangles. The windows are stately, I don't know why the windows are so important here, the wooden window casings are themselves embedded in striking granite frames. The railings around the stairs, the floor is gouged by canals, grooves, red spirals, and brass rods that keep the carpet taut against the folds of the staircase. Railings, banisters, polished snails at the end of stone waterfalls on either side of the slide of steps.

We go up to that floor and walk down the hallway. The window at the end shows only light; we are above the treetops. We don't speak, so as not to get caught. Anticipation.

She, of course, is a virgin. And I press down on that barrier with the whole weight of my body, as if poured into a funnel. A whirlpool that changes my own anatomy: at the very bottom, in the center, the point that I flow through—this is where my heart is. And my belly button as well, and maybe even some steaming spot on my back has been sucked down into this vortex. While up above, all at once my head, legs, and bangs are the leftover silt in the funnel.

She is a virgin, of course, but why is she not wearing panties under her skirt? And that vulgar smile—in her eyes, not on her lips. I, too, am a virgin, perhaps in a more concrete or more specific sense—both of us realize our innocence at the same moment, but of the two of us there's one who senses that . . .

>>>

Here, in short, is what I want to find out, what I want to clarify in this split-second before the memory is shattered by that internal explosion between two bodies: is that gaze really there, the eyes in that portrait above me, on the wall of the quiet dusky hall we tiptoed into? We're naked now, her skirt hiked up, my pants down around my knees, shirt unbuttoned. Who is watching us?

But no matter how quickly everything was over, according to the prescription of nature and the summary procedure of the moment, it turns out that time itself, chronology, does not exhaust—and can never exhaust—the energy hidden in the body. Even years later, most probably in my imagination or perhaps not quite, I found myself forced again and again to bend over that body, her body, the object of this coupling, in order to understand. A body that could be the joyful center of my very self, of my very own *I*. The mirror of my masculinity, if it didn't represent above all the risk of being accused of a crime.

So that, in short, is what I want to figure out. That's the very core I'm trying to reach: she is still a part of *his* body and he is present in hers. What could K-shev's gaze mean here, because in the dream I didn't know his name, since she hadn't yet told me, nor his significance, since at that moment I was still a naïve Pioneer. And now for the explanation: why is it that if you cross out a name, if you have the nerve to repeal it, to change your own family name—why does that still add up to nothing but vain attempts and wasted efforts? The body, the flesh does not play by those rules. The body, the flesh transforms itself according to its own laws.

That's why this story has turned into such a bodily adventure— no connection is more bodily than inheritance, which makes up the whole of you, yet which you also desperately want to get rid of more than anything. I think that here on the Reeperbahn, in Hamburg, Germany, there is no way to prevent bodies from playing their role. You can couple with bodies, but you can't run from them. They always get in your way. In the end, you have no choice but to *go through*.

In this case, I really wasn't prepared—for the Reeperbahn in Hamburg, that is. My premature exit from the booth and that unfinished scene, which was like the graphic truth about coupling—but without the increasing tenderness, just flesh and color. An act that is far too bodily.

The same problem yet again—the body. I didn't want to tear my eyes away, but I had to run, I had to get the hell out of there.

>>>

In an ironic twist of fate, K-shev is now dying of cancer in this sterile, private German clinic—as much as it may look like a hospital, it's obviously little more than a very expensive hospice. The still-breathing corpses lie inside, while outside nobody waits for them anymore. At best, a battle is raging to divide the spoils.

In this case everything was gathered into a small, thin briefcase.

It was a brand-new briefcase, or at least it was new when they put it in the safety deposit box in the bank vault. A very well-insulated place, that vault—I can vouch for that now that I've brought the briefcase back to my hotel room and can still catch a scent of new leather, as if it had been bought only yesterday.

To kill time, I measured its height, width, and depth with a pack of cigarettes: 1 x 5 x 3, more or less.

Just as he told me, there is more than a million inside. I've never seen so much money in one place. But besides this cliché, I can also tell you that there is nothing *optically* unusual about this huge amount of cash. Or maybe I was already numb, perhaps my senses were dulled like his from the life-support machines whirring away behind the doors lining the white corridors. You absorb old people's anesthesia by induction, the opiate of medication, the opiate of age.

He needs the money now, needs it with a fatal urgency, whether his brain realizes it or not. I made sure to confirm this as soon as I arrived. I thought the place would be disgusting, but it was only strangely arid, sterile, quiet. I didn't experience any revulsion, impatience, or rage. I didn't feel anything at all *inside* myself, only on the surface. Instead of the torturous spasm of my whole being that I expected, I experienced only a bodily discomfort, as if I were wearing the wrong-sized clothes or too-tight shoes.

I was uncomfortable in the white hospital chair; my back was to the window and the potted plant next to it. It looked dried out, pressed in an album, even though it was still alive; I even caught the slightly tangy scent of its leaves and the sweetish odor of withering and decay. A hospital room, a room for death. I'm wondering if I shouldn't look into the old man's eyes to see: is he thinking about the end?

When I got back after going to the bank, I went straight into the bathroom, undressed, and filled up the tub. Afterward I stood for a long time under the shower. I wanted my body to soften up; it was like some kind of shell had crusted onto me—I know this was just my imagination, but the scrubbing did me good and I no longer saw myself in the fogged-up mirror. Just a huge profusion of bottles in the white steam, little flasks of monochromatic creamy liquids, all in twenty-gram doses for hotel junkies. I didn't feel like going out yet, so I examined them—most had Italian labels. Care of the body, it seems, carries a whiff of the exotic and distant. No matter whether they're made in Hong Kong or here, the labels must be in a foreign language—what are people thinking when they choose their dreams? Money is definitely a crucial element. Okay, well here's the money, I've got it. What happens now?

Yes, the money was already on the table when I left the bathroom, stepping barefoot onto the soft carpet. Water dripped all around me as I stood in the center of the room, my head was spinning ever so slightly from the heat, from exhaustion, from the red-eye flight, from impatience to do the deed and from the wavering question mark lodged in my stomach: Why did I do it? Do I even understand what I'm doing now? Do I have to do this? Is it right? Does it mean I'm responsible, that by doing this the blood is on my hands?

Then I flopped down on the still-made bed. The bedspread was clean, but somehow shabby. Sterilized and ostensibly normal, yet with my body's expanded and cleansed pores I sensed its lack of coziness, overcrowded with reminders of previous guests, sleeping bodies. Of course, all this turned my thoughts back to the hospital, or perhaps it was the opposite: I continued to be there in my mind, until in the end the bed itself from room 308 at the Hotel Hamburg actually began to move toward Krankenstrasse—or better, Krankenhausstrasse—in any case, it was moving toward that *Strasse* as if toward a test point where I can check with a simple physical touch whether I really am moving or whether I'm dreaming under hypnosis, or both, or most likely some third possibility, or whether I really am fighting my way toward the goal I have set for myself.

>>>

I began to entertain the thought of saying "to hell with all this" and going out and having fun with *his* money. Whatever *his* means is a different story, but now isn't the time for that, not tonight.

Right then, that night, at 8 P.M. as I left the Hotel Hamburg, I was sure that this long day would end by midnight at the latest and with a girl, paid for with cash. Or better yet, with two hired girls. And I would pay them more than I had to, because it would be his money. The booth with the red ceiling and the neon lights was merely a rehearsal. So that I would later be able to last longer with real girls, with prostitutes—I'm not going to come fast, I told myself. And so on.

Those were my plans at eight.

>>>

It is worth noting that this city, with one foot in the sea and the other in the river, has strange pigeons. At first, you mistake them for northern seagulls, but they are actually pigeons, they have a white or dark gray ring around the neck. A sign of something familiar, native, like back home. Here's the other thing that made an impression on me: As I was wandering around at night, next to the manicured green lawns on either side of the navigation canal, I saw light shadows jumping on the grass. Because of their size, I first thought they were rabbits. But then I saw that they were rats, nonchalantly passing by on some path of their own. Hamburg—a river town, a sea town, northern and very rich. Rats, prostitutes, and the Reeperbahn: they didn't give the impression of seediness, but quite the opposite, the feeling of stable Saxon comfort, which made it almost fitting to pay for pleasure with his money.

Of course, when I think about that money, the pleasure can only fade, nothing more.

I couldn't give in that easily, however. I tried to find somebody to blame: the mechanized environment, the change machine, the video player that projected the films on the screen, those monotonous doors, too, and the neon light, the apathetic or overexcited faces, the silhouettes lingering by the windows—the whole disturbing yet quintessentially German erotic system, from which you expect at least a little more chaos, but no. All of these tiny elements pile up like obstacles, speed bumps against accelerating sensitivity, and instead of awakening more excitement, they arouse thought above all. And in the end, maybe even some pangs of conscience, and a little fear.

>>>

Hamburg, early or late. Love is already laid out on the autopsy table. I'm becoming more and more alarmed. Am I ruining my life? Just a month ago, even a week ago I still could've turned back. But now I've made my move, I've rolled the dice. I think some parts of my body are rolling around with them, my head definitely is. Somebody else is calling the shots and making decisions instead of me, someone who looks like me, but in a different form and a different phase, somewhere in the past. That's why I've started to trust that somebody more. But if it turns out that the path from here on out leads me to some final abyss, the figure of that somebody won't be solid enough; it will disintegrate, leaving me disagreeably alone. Whom will I blame then, who will be the guilty one?

I turn back the clock, then quickly wind it forward, and then back again. I take one of the bundles: new, smooth bills, all hundreds, a hundred times a hundred in a light-blue wrapper. I fan through the stack, the paper passes quickly under my fingers and the identical edges repeat themselves. No motion at all, suspended animation. The silhouette of a bridge reflected in water smacks into the reflections on the bills above it. There are no pedestrians on the bridge, the map in the lower corner is too general, too empty. Where is Hamburg on that map, where am I on Seewartenstrasse, in a gray concrete citadel-hotel on the shore, wrapped in night and glass? The thought of going down to the lobby gives me the chills, but the dangerous thing is that I don't even know why. I got mixed up in something I had no right to mess with; touching this money, I smell the scent of the leather coffin it was put into, ready for burial. In fact, I was this close to throwing it into the dark waters of the harbor. To the rats. To the girls in the bluish outfits, leaning on eighteenth century façades up there on the street called Reeperbahn. A strange slice of the city's history, where the rope makers used to spread out bales of hemp to braid kilometers of rope, reaching as far as the city gates. It would be a naïve lie, however, one you wouldn't believe, if I told you that I blame some other noose, and not the noose I'm tightening within myself. How did I end up here? Not accidentally, of course. Even if there were coincidences and chaotic stabs into the flesh of fate, I nevertheless said "yes."

Money frightens, that's another one of its characteristics: it arouses fear. It's as if its very origins evoke crime, despite the bank's guarantee of cleanliness. The more money, the more suspicion.

I sit up, get to my feet, put on my sunglasses, and pause in front of the mirror hanging on the wallpapered wall of room 308, Hotel Hamburg. Who do you look like now? Am I sufficiently suspicious looking? Obviously not to the girls lounging in their usual places on Davidstrasse, who readily toss invitations my way:

"*Komm schon, Blondy!*"

"*Komm schon, wir machen es französisch!*"

>>>

The docks of Hamburg, on the banks of the Elba, the largest pontoon structure in Europe. St. Michael's Tower with its four clocks—the tallest clock tower in Europe. I don't dare fix my gaze there for long, on the home of the Archangel, so instead my eyes follow the smaller mast of light, the white clock faces. They shine straight at me: the harbor tower. Where should I sail away to?

I get dressed. I don't have the right clothes or storm gear to stand proudly on the deck. I have nowhere to sail to now, so it wouldn't make any sense. I know what I have to do this morning, at dawn: run.

Running is a forgotten pleasure, but that's not the point now; we're talking about survival. About escape—running usually turns out to be the path to it. The only difference is the starting and ending points—from what or from whom, and to where and why am I running?—everything is still unclear.

I don't care if I look ridiculous in my hiking boots and too-short shorts verging on Speedos. I don't glance at the professional maniacs who start while it's still dark, I pass them by as if they're shadows stuck inside fancy three-ply runner's gear made of revolutionary fibers. I'm hopelessly sweaty, dark wet stains appear in my armpits and on my back. I don't have a hat or a visor or earphones to sway to some rhythm like those sports zombies on the paths. They pass, meet, and go around me because I don't swerve, I run in a straight line. A tall German with his two-meter-long strides tries to pass me—I don't think so, my friend. You may not realize it, but I can tolerate pain. My heels are burning, my socks are twisting around my shins. My gait is aggressive, ugly, but I keep an enviable distance—see ya' later, sucker!—and he turns off, as if he'd been planning to go that way all along, to avoid defeat. Because he can't pass me. Now that I've gone into sprint mode, there's no turning back. Full speed ahead. Sweat pours down, gluing my eyelids shut, drenching my eyebrows—I can't see and have no idea where I'm going, but the running continues, I run and run.

>>>

From control point CP-9 to control point CP-8
I had this dream with my eyes wide open: wilderness orientation.
Pioneer camp. A Spec Ops orienteering race through the woods, the thick grass in the rain. Xenon, the camp dog, a big, black German shepherd, zigzags left and right, but—thanks to his border-guard genes—doesn't bark.

We run around using compasses to search for invisible lines, azimuths, hidden among the trees. Once we guess the direction, we discover orientation signs, concealed by pine boughs. A cardboard sign reading "CP-8"—there is a small map and a symbol, our goal is marked with a colorful arrow. Around my waist, under my T-shirt, our team's flag is twisted and tied into a knot. We pass it around, taking turns carrying it. The fake silk soaks up the childish salt of our sweat. Now, in my memory I notice that despite the sweat and grime, my body gave off no scent. And so . . .

. . . woods, pines, firs. Cedars. Sharp green needles and wide leaves. We run over the silent moss, in step, our knees and shins scratched from the still-soft milk teeth of wild roses, of blackberry bushes. Our elbows and shoulders stinging from the little whips of jutting branches, the thick hazel trees. And all of a sudden amid the bottomless green: a dark blue spot, movement with a persistent color.

Strange white shoes, hair swinging in a ponytail. One moving spot, and another one right next to it. I saw her.

Wilderness orientation—from CP-7 to CP-6
I lost sight of the vision. The ghost born of entangled, blinking eyelashes flew away quickly, like a bird amid the branches. At least that's how it seemed to me. It's just a game, there's no real danger here. Pioneer camp, a children's war, the running continues.

We reached the river—we crossed without fording, with quick steps across the stones. Under the thin rubber soles of your tennis shoes you can feel the edges of the rocks, splashes of water cool you off momentarily. And again running, quickened breath—where is the mirage, the blue spot on green infinity? The bouncing braid, the white heels of the odd shoes, which still had their strange treads—look, there they are here—leaving unfamiliar tracks.

We reach a long curve, encircling the slope bristling with trees. The dank shade raises goose bumps on our bare arms. Who is waiting for us around the corner?

An April rain begins to fall.

\>\>\>

Raindrops glistened through the sunshine, fluff floated from the poplars, crossing into the rain's line of fire.

My eyes swim from so much blonde hair, girls in blue blouses. My head starts to spin. A strange taste invades my lungs, the scent of ozone—what does ozone smell like anyway?—at least that's what I tell myself now as I try to grasp something more, a greater meaning and importance held in those last few moments.

And the question I add to all this today: why didn't anybody call out to us, tell us to come back? So many secrets in such a short time, in the seconds before I fainted for no good reason.

"From exhaustion and too much running," as the Pioneer camp doctor dryly declared afterward. Okay—before I dropped from exhaustion into the soft blades of the tall grass. Before the kaleidoscopic reflections of the girls' ghostly silhouettes accumulated into a single body.

The sky above my head widened, filled my eyes, and I fell into it, fell into the rain, into something huge and blue, not black like they usually say the color of collapse is.

"From exhaustion and too much running," repeats the doctor and gives me an injection in the arm.

"No!"—I feel like shouting—but my voice slips into weightlessness at the edge of my throat.

"You didn't see anything," the comforting voices repeat, the needle pulls out of my skin.

"It was nothing, nobody, you're imagining it," I hear, or rather dream, that they're speaking to me.

"Shh, shh, go to sleep"—the last thing I can make out is the voice of the scout leader: "Go to sleep, dream"—the warmth of a hand on my chest. The warmth of the sun still at its zenith, while I fall asleep too early, exceptionally early. A cotton ball with a drop of rubbing alcohol on it raises a silent toast to the tiny puncture where the mixture of beneficent poison and healing sleep has entered. Time passes, the minute and hour hands can't hold me. The clocks on all sides of the tower spin. Now I can see in all four cardinal directions, too, but I can't seem to move in a single one of them.

Uranus

The control point is the smallest possible space that can contain the ultimate goal—or just the temporary goal—of this leg of the race, the searching and finding, the blazing of a trail in this thick impenetrable forest. So what's the function of the meadow, then? A place to rest and to play or a ruse, a trap set by strange forces? Clever bait to draw you out of the forest and into the open, so that the eyes of spy satellites can see you from invisible heights? Or so the radioactive rain can fall on you?

We had no way of knowing, it wasn't marked on the map and no dosimetric lines were drawn on the orienteering stencil—a few days earlier, a thousand kilometers to the north and east, Reactor No. 4 at Chernobyl had exploded, under the watch of the Fifth Shift. The pioneer camp commander later summed it up with his favorite saying: "Shit happens."

Letter to an Unknown Comrade

I know, my dear, little, unknown Soviet and Ukrainian comrade, I know, but please—don't finish yet, tell me again. Tell me how it happened once more, tell me, even if it means repeating yourself and wasting yet another whole page of graph paper. For me it's important, it's so important, you can't even begin to imagine.

I want to hear about the banks of the Pripyat River—I can see its water boiling, I understand. But more about that later, it's still too early, April hasn't arrived yet, nor the beginning of May, the water is calm. Longer ago and further back, before spring and before winter. Tell me about the summer, the past, as if there never was and never will be one like it again, as if it were the last. As if we are running for the last time with pounding carefree steps toward the banks, toward the water, and it flows smoothly from the tributaries and empties out into the Dnieper. Show me around the flat terrain, across those 106,000 square kilometers, geographically, like a straight-A student. There, where the water-drainage basin stretches past the nuclear power plant. Scribble on the map, all along the river's 748 kilometers with a black marker. Give me a little more time. I'm playing here in the grass, it's raining, my dear little unknown comrade from the Pale between Ukraine and Belarus—I'm not even exactly sure where you are, on the map in my textbook that little corner is too small, between two holes of the spiral binding that hold the pages together. So tell me about it now, give me time to stand here a little longer, in the rain.

In return, let me admit that you are now extending this moment in Paradise—she is blonde, my little Soviet comrade from Ukraine, from Belarus, she is a blue T-shirt and blonde hair in braids and shoes with a strange design on the heels. Tell me whatever you want, don't make me ask, my lips are busy, my words are busy. I put a lot of effort into my Russian, see how beautifully I write to you with loops and hooks, correctly using the instrumental case and the backward "e," right?

While here with her, we can't utter a single word, so we just move, we move and breathe.

Don't ask me why or what for, just close your eyes and tell me, like you used to write me. Tell me again about the Pripyat River, about its waters. I know they're brown because those waters flow from *Geography*, from peat-bogs. And if you want to swim, you'd better be strong because the current will sweep you away. After swimming, a coating like chocolate covers your skin, it tightens, dries out, and bakes in the air—if you pick at it with your fingers it squeaks. Like a festive Misha the Olympian, one of those marzipan bears sold as an Olympic souvenir. Of course, you know that it's because of the swamp acids, which must be good for you—even fish swim in and breathe them. But *after the disaster* they will turn into coagulating agents, as the nuclear physicists call them, since they are excellent conveyors of radioactive particles, the leftovers from the breakdown of the spilled nuclear fuel, God damn it, as the nuclear physicists, or "nukies," swore through their teeth. You are probably the child of a nukie, my dear little unknown comrade—otherwise what would you be doing in that city built in the middle of nowhere? In the middle of the Pale, there and where else in that emptiness would you be born, at that unremarkable age, the same age as the fourth reactor, the pride of the golden five-year-plans for energy construction.

You are probably a nukie's child, because you know, your daddy told you—when he didn't prefer to stay silent, when he said that he was just coming home for a bit and then would have to go back— that the whole power plant was leaking. It was leaking like crazy, God damn it, the nukies cursed, it was leaking, the whole thing was just one leak after another, somewhere in the ballpark of fifty cubic meters an hour through the faltering reinforcement, through the drains. Fifty cubic meters of radioactive water an hour, my boy, my dear little Soviet boy—even I know that's a lot. The vaporizers can hardly process it. Radioactive oversaturation, as they say, and they very often send your dad on radioactive business trips, all the way to the great country's capital, to that special Sixth Moscow Clinic. God damn it—but there's no cure for this exhaustion, he's always falling asleep at the table, head on the tablecloth, facedown amid the cherry jam and slices of bread. That's a gift from our native fields—so I'm there in the picture, too. You don't know it, my dear little comrade, but I was on the work brigade at the jam factory. That very jar, cherry jam, with a pit.

It's very easy for them to blame him, to call him an idiot, a drunk or an ideological freak, depending on the audience and the depth of the argument required. But, my dear little comrade, I know—daddies never do anything without thinking about their children. Or even without asking them. The disguised Father Christmas makes every child's dreams come true.

So let them write, let them compile lists that pedantically point out oversights, let them count off at length the failures to conform to labor standards and operating procedures, to the Energy Code, to the material and moral principles for acting in zones of elevated radioactive risk—oversights, mistakes, and unimplemented security measures of primary importance. And in brief, including only the gravest errors, for example, the following: that the workers on the fifth shift shut down the emergency system, they stopped and started the machine however they saw fit, doing the same with the automatic regulation system. And what's this talk of cooling turbines, given that for the purposes of this strange experiment all the backup energy sources were cut off and even sealed off in advance—let's see what'll happen, those sharp minds said, let's just see.

And what happened? The temperature rose highly strangely and strangely high, somehow quite perceptibly. The reactor, of course, was itself a Party member, it didn't want to explode and humiliate the great country, its scientists and academics, who shouted all the livelong day that the Soviet atom was the safest atom on the planet—the reactor resisted, wringing its hands, trying desperately to keep itself together. But here the masters of that deadly sport had already put it in a headlock that no one could escape from—not even Reactor Four of the world's third-largest atomic power plant (both in terms of size and capacity), which is even described in the Apocalypse.

And the control system, the control system designed precisely for such cases, was frozen up in any case—on top of everything the leaders of the experiment themselves, engineers, scientists, physicists, had turned it off earlier so that it wouldn't get in the way of their plans. And so, with its back against the wall, with access to all emergency generators cut off—the two diesel generators as well as the two electrical transformers—the block, the reactor was stranded above the abyss without any energy except *atomic* energy. Without energy to stop, that is.

And finally—sometime around 1:20 in the morning—finally when their hair began to stand on end because they realized that they were pulling the levers of a fuse measuring fourteen meters in diameter and seven meters tall, filled with toasty, warm uranium—funny, hadn't they realized it before?—no, apparently not, alas—then they just threw up their hands and cried "Mommy!" But Mommy was nowhere to be found, so they pulled the fatal lever labeled ES: "Emergency Shield."

Which allowed the incompetence of the reactor's constructors and builders to come into play. Because some of the control rods had somehow been designed incorrectly, but who bothered about that, anyway? And who would've thought that those rods would ever need to enter the heart of the reactor with a crash, in such a state of wild panic—according to the regulations, they should never have even been taken out at all! And so on and so forth—an endless stream of mutual accusations and justifications between the builders, users, enemies, and friends of peaceful nuclear power for Soviet aims.

I know there are no longer birches, poplars, a city, houses, Lenin Street, the school; the 50,000 inhabitants have disappeared somewhere. But my dear little Soviet comrade, I still keep your address, I write you letters that never arrive—just so you know that I am eternally grateful to your father and to all those fathers who, despite the efforts of the control system, managed to blow the reactor sky-high. To blow *me* sky-high.

>>>

I, unlike everyone else, do not blame K-shev for not warning us. I don't care—I have unique personal memories, historical ones. For me, Chernobyl is a flash of a moment that surpasses all moments worthy of the name "epic." Like the eureka light bulb going off in Edison's skull: the day you understand everything without needing to think.

I already know—now, later, after reading all those books, all those declassified documents. I, as they say, bless the right hand of the creators of those uranium-graphite reactors, with all of their thoughtlessness. The greatness of scientists is not measured by some abstract perfection—on the contrary, it is measured by their talent to make a predicted mistake. To hide it in a system of complicated formulas and terminology so as to remain invisible to small-minded Party leaders.

My brothers, may it be strong as ore,
that blessed right hand of yours—
with the valiant Reactor Four
you lit up a star!

>>>

"We trusted the experts' evaluations," they whisper on the upper floors, hidden in offices behind oak doors, huddled in corners near the trashcans. "All for the good of the people and the working class"—nodding, the participants in the Party schools explain this to one another, smoking during breaks, and come to an agreement with insulting ease. Comrade K-shev is somewhere among them, a guest in the great Soviet nation, sent by a small tomato republic, with his pompadour and hand-knit sweater vest. Sent on business from a quiet little country poised to soon become yet another car in the bullet-train—right after the end of lessons in mastering solidarity.

"We . . ." a slightly guilty and listless voice begins a summary over a radio loudspeaker that is somewhat sagging, yet well-slathered with paint just like the wallpaper and doorframe in the yellowish-dusky color of the era.

Now I realize why the hallways are so empty as she and I creep through them—the stairways, the corners, the railings, the mirrors without reflections in them, the crimson curtains and the empty pedestals. They are all at a meeting. They are making important decisions.

"We trusted the scientists," they sniffle into the loudspeaker, passing around the responsibility like lice in a kindergarten. They squint an eye, pick at the ugly guts of this wart—an imaginary one, of course, yet still dangerous, even twice as dangerous for its imaginariness. What did you inadvertently touch in the pandemonium? Why are you still wiping your fingers on the curtains—to get rid of the invisible contagion of fear—could it be that *something has happened*? That something has finally happened to you.

"We carried out our orders. We met the deadlines."

"The bosses, the Party . . . the Congress . . ."

K-shev remains silent, however; he doesn't justify himself to anyone. There's something I like about the guy, something that excites me to a particularly strange, radioactive degree, especially at the moment when I bury my fingers in the milky-blue, fleshy-cloth combination of the pleated skirt and naked thighs of his daughter.

He revolves around the axis of his own unshakable foundation, built over the void. It'll only take a bit more to convince me, just a bit more. Just some extra gesture, accidental, seemingly trivial, that will let me know that he is not simply a Party flunky, but *divine*. He doesn't need to run from responsibility because he is in a completely different relationship to responsibility itself. He himself is the creator of responsibilities.

Strangely, his illness now seems at first glance like a failure, a tumble from the altar I was prepared to place him on. But perhaps this is only at first glance—for this reason I'm not rushing to pity him so easily; I've seen many falls. Could the illness be the final proof I need to deify him once and for all? A strange sort of god, ready to die even—from an illness no less, one we ourselves all feared becoming infected with. Is he capable of such an act purely and solely to win our faith?

>>>

There, there, my dear little Soviet comrade: don't cry, don't be sad, don't change your surname, don't be ashamed of your name. Take flowers to your daddy's grave, even though only a blue suit with metal buttons is buried there. After the hydrogen-oxygen explosion at the reactor, fueled by uranium dioxide UO_2 on a bed of zirconium, under the skeleton of niobium—nothing was left of the bodies.

"But we did everything just as we were supposed to"—only evaporated ghosts repeat these words now.

"We did everything correctly, following the established plan approved by the management!" Just as under socialism—we do and did everything correctly, yet life, the world, continues to collapse beneath our feet like a reactor that has entered a runaway state of nuclear meltdown. Is there any need to explain what those two great liberating words mean: *chain reaction*?

A reaction that breaks chains. Indeed, freedom is equal in strength to the truth. But first the opposite had to happen.

And I had to come across his daughter, of course.

>>>

K-shev watches me from the framed black-and-white photograph. Only in the meaning of that gaze, in the subsections of the ideological tract can I search for the true foundations. The sick passion that firmly grips and envelops both our bodies—mine and *his daughter's*. It changes from tenderness into exertion, from exertion into force, into tension to the point of pain: power.

At the end, as usual, the tempo should speed up, just a bit more and everything is over. The moment of the happy ending, the verge of that thirsting absurdity. But that is precisely the moment when I can throw a wrench in the spokes of natural progression, of desire: I slow the beating of my heart, the throbbing of blood in the basement of my organism, the boiling of seething lava. All internal muscles push and jerk, hopelessly trying to overcome the built-up ballast—but I resist, working against them.

I'm pretty vile, that's clear—I'm obviously depraved. Because I keep a dark and repulsive memory like a worn-out old photograph in my hand. And at the decisive moment, under cover of a final cherished kiss, of a free fusion of lips—I paste it *onto her face*.

The whole horror of experiencing communism, or socialism—call it what you will—hangs gaping in all its absurdity if you don't manage to do the most important thing: reach the body of *the daughter*. And best of all—the daughter of K-shev himself.

The Year 2000, a Morning at the End of the Century

"I had a really weird dream," I tell her.

"It doesn't matter," she responds. She's doing her hair.

"I dreamed I was running."

"You don't have time to jog this morning." She doesn't turn around; she's completely absorbed in winding and twisting something around her hair.

"I was running really fast, faster than ever before."

"Well, it's not gonna happen. You'll have to skip your run today. Come on, get up, get dressed."

I keep silent. I could tell her everything, I feel like I could tell her absolutely everything. And she wouldn't turn away, she'd hear me out, and at the end she'd rest her head on my forehead, I'm sure of it. She'd run her fingers through my hair, like she loves to, she would start doing my hair with the same concentration she gives her own.

They love me—I'm not sure why that is, what I'm made of— but they fall very easily and deeply in love with me, and afterward I practically have to pry them off with a crowbar. As a result, love becomes my primary enemy. I'm not saying it's normal, I'm not normal at all. I'm not proud of this, I'm probably a freak—but they get used to that, too. They ask you questions, hammering away at you, yelling, in the end they accept it and just ask out of inertia without expecting a concrete answer, "Just tell me what you want. I don't get it."

What they count on most is the complexity of male desires. It's hard to answer the general question: what do you want? So I answer very concretely, using names, weights and colors: "I want coffee and doughnuts"—this snaps the passive listener out of her stupor. "*What?*" is the following logical and slightly astonished question.

"Coffee and doughnuts, but with that taste of the good old days."

The effect of sincerity is short-lived. They soon turn their back on you again, somehow accusingly, but now with a certain contempt. Women are at first endlessly curious, they start to love me. Then they begin to despise me to my very core, because I turn out to be boring, the living picture of their dissatisfaction. Should I ask them what they wanted from me or whether I've promised anything? I don't think there's any point.

>>>

"Come on, get up, wake up! How can you even feel like sleeping, I could hardly sleep a wink from anxiety."

What anxiety, I could reply, but I don't want to. Some breath of the dream is caught between my lips, a warm sip with a strange aftertaste, slightly bitter, slightly sweet, the slightly rotten taste of waking that spurs you to brush your teeth—so as to forget that gloomy little ghost, that telltale memory, trace, souvenir and hint that in your dreams you embraced something dead.

"You haven't shown me anything of your father's," I say after swallowing that chunk of mummified dream.

I lie back on the pillow. She has stopped moving her hand, right as it was passing through the roots of her hair. I love watching women stop moving their hands, especially when executing one of the most primitive female movements.

"What?"

"It just occurred to me all of a sudden, I don't know why, that you almost never say anything about your father."

"My father's been gone for years, you know that."

"He died."

I say this without a questioning intonation, yet not exactly as a statement, either. More like an opinion open to argument, proof, verification or refutation.

"What's the matter with you?" Her nervous liveliness has suddenly dried up. After that I again hear in her voice those notes of annoyance and stubbornness. The feeling that she's being attacked—by none other than me. "Did something happen? Are you trying to tell me something?"

I keep silent. She reaches out her hand toward mine:

"Come on, get up."

But I don't move.

>>>

How did I meet her? Our whole shared path has passed under the banner of tension. I can't understand why, I can't even recognize myself.

"Get up, get dressed."

I remain silent in response.

She leans over me threateningly:

"I'm not going to let you do this."

"You go ahead, leave me alone."

"That's not going to happen."

"I said leave me alone!"

We fall easily into a childish squabble. Only I can't remember what we're fighting about, as usual. There was some theme, some attempt to outwit each other. A childish war always flares up over some formal reason, but the symbolism of the toy, the object under dispute, is usually deeper, much deeper. Like an unconscious motif, for example, a lack of parental love, more precisely a father's love. I strike again while I know the wound has not yet healed:

"Tell me about your father and I promise to get up right away."

The glass alarm clock in its see-through case rings near my head—I don't have time to close my eyes, to protect myself, she hurls it at me from very close range. She didn't even pick it up in her hand, just swatted at it with her open palm and it smashed against the wall, shattering into pieces.

With eyes now closed, as I overcome the fear of a potential new blow, I continue. So cold and calm that I am amazed at my own voice:

"Tell me about him and you'll feel better. We'll both feel better. We'll make peace. You'll make peace with yourself."

A much-needed pause. Silence.

"I'm not going to let you do this," she speaks the words very quietly, but very clearly, right over my head.

I open my eyes. I see her directly above me. She's looking at me vertically, her gaze like a plumb line, in its lower part her irises are hidden under the edges of her lower eyelids.

>>>

How did I find her? I don't think it was a matter of choice. Every moment of my communication with her is actually movement toward the very moment when she will strip herself naked, like a steel blade unsheathed, and the true reasons will blaze forth. The more I resist, the longer and more cruelly the blade will be sharpened, raised like a scorpion's tail, ready to strike.

"I had a really weird dream," I tell her, to soften her up, at least to start.

"It doesn't matter," she replies and makes the first move, just like every other time.

Just like every other time, first a drop of childish blood is shed, in the sense that she makes me suffer through all my childish scorching-enchanting memories all over again. We reach this stage easily—we need only to start the familiar game. In the game, she is never his daughter, as it were. Total disguise, total relief, total flight from the reality of whose daughter she actually is.

His

They only make such an effort for the children of the Party elites. Black cars, no motorcade. They bring the boys and girls there as inconspicuously as possible, at dawn. The children are sleepy, they don't resist. The medical checkup has to take place in a semi-dream state.

The building is surrounded by woods, you can hear the birds. The stone path leads up to the entrance, now is a convenient time, Sunday, the whole complex is empty. At the entrance: only the guard.

They lead her into a changing room and point to the hook. She takes off her skirt, her shoes, her T-shirt cut low under the arms—they all wear those, both boys and girls. She's left only in her panties.

"Don't be afraid," the doctor with the horn-rimmed glasses tells her, a professor of something or other, and the woman has her lie down on a metal stretcher in front of a strange machine. She isn't actually a woman, but rather a pudgy man; below the elbow his arms have the same meaty, twisted flab as on the arms of the cleaning lady whom she sees every morning at home with her mop and bucket in the hallway in front of her father's office. This strange man-woman's hair is hidden under a white cap, just like the lady who gives out rolls and pours warm milk from a teapot later in the morning at school.

They don't have school for a few days, so they don't have snacks during recess. They brought different food and milk in a jar, frothy and very sour—this is the way it has to be, they told her, you mustn't eat anything else. The wild plums of springtime, the wild cherries in the courtyard of the residence—everything was forbidden. Vacation, they told her, but not at the seaside—you can't go to the seaside, now isn't a good time for the seaside.

"Don't be afraid," the doctor of something or other tells her, "we're just going to measure something, we'll check something, it won't hurt." The steel frame of the stretcher and its brown leather hammock start moving slowly. She slides along, lying on top of it, she slides toward a towering lead pyramid in the center of the room, the walls are painted a very light blue, it's enough to make your head spin and your eyes ache. The pyramid is made up of fat gray rectangles. Her legs are swallowed up with a hissing sound from the electric motor, her body slowly slides forward. She wants to close her eyes, but she can't, not before reaching the mountain of lead.

"See," says the doctor, trying to speak in a fairytale voice and failing miserably, "you'll just pass through this little tunnel and that's it. It'll just take a minute, long enough for us to measure something, and then you'll come out the other side. There's nothing to be afraid of, it won't hurt a bit, I promise."

It must weigh a ton, it must weigh two or ten or a hundred tons even, that mountain, that pyramid. What is it and what's going on?—no one tells her, no one can explain it to her. There's no way to quickly and easily explain the function and principle behind the workings of the gamma spectrometer with lead shields, the electro-radiation scanner, the isotope identifier . . .

Just a year or two later the girl would become dangerous. Because children ask questions when they grow up.

>>>

I know she has memories she doesn't share with me. That's where she's hidden the hate, along with the cause and the reason. I still haven't asked her, I haven't even hinted at *his money*, I pretend that it would never even cross my mind. I'm interested in her body alone, it's the only thing I'm possessive of.

Today they want to condemn K-shev, as if he were an illness—the charges have been brought under an article from the Health Act. They try him in absentia, of course, because he's not there. I'm also absent, even though I'm a potential witness.

Do you remember that rain, that radioactive rain?, they could ask me.

The rain? Yes, I remember it, but look, I'd feel like telling them, by a twist of fate he's now dying of cancer. What's the point? The judgment has already been pronounced on some symbolic level.

I could find more and more dull topics to hush up the main one, to keep my hidden goal and secret safe. But no one hears me, because I don't actually talk, I'm silent. I haven't been summoned. She orders me to get dressed, to finally get up. Maybe she wants—in a fit of hatred toward her father—dreams of going to the courtroom, of supporting the prosecutor's accusations. But I don't get up, I stubbornly resist. And why, you ask? I've got plans of my own, heh heh!

There's no use trying to convince me, I'm sure there are memories she hasn't shared with me. The longer sincerity is put off, the more vicious the use of the lips becomes—not for speaking, but for biting. The descent into speechlessness deepens. I hope that we'll finally start talking, at least before we definitively and fatally harm ourselves.

The radio is on, the prosecutor's accusations continue. Willing and unwilling semi-guilty semi-idiots, witnesses and participants line up. They dump onto K-shev the remnants of their memories, along with the remnants of their responsibility. The primary defendant's absence is just so convenient, he has no way to speak for himself. The experts pedantically rehash the chronology. They point to data, numbers in tables. The Party crumbles into pieces, disintegrates into atoms—just as it did then.

April-May 1986

In the party headquarters of the reactor, in the reactor of the party headquarters—foreign gazes invade the pried-off lid. The whole world already knows everything, only we remain in the dark. Malaysia returns shipments of milk imported from Poland. Sparks and telegrams fly between capital cities around the world. Moscow finally, grudgingly confesses. Kiev is in mourning, albeit unofficially. But Sofia stays silent, the spring unfolds panic-free.

Is there anyone else out there who still gets heated up by these decades-old memories? Is it only the two of us, me and her? While decomposing, we leave naked bodies behind—during brief collapses they quiver from the scalding stray sparks.

A hand—impossible to tell whose, mine or hers—hits upon the island of the nightstand. In the first second I don't know what for: gauze, cotton, or a Band-Aid, or a canister of ethyl chloride, because there are times when the skin itself can't take anymore, so it has to be numbed. With the scent of evaporating gas from the glass balloon, all the questions come out. What prevented Comrade K-shev from informing the population on time? What, for God's sake?

But I don't care. I'm radiating rays, I'm lit up. Glittering nucleotides bursting from my body in all directions. The water tastes unbelievably bitter in my mouth, the stinging air envelops my hands, all the hairs standing on end in my skin shoot out arrows. Butterflies fall all around me, along with stunned spring sparrows, the frogs in the marshes don't finish their jet-propelled jumps. The water fleas, legs splayed on the surface of the pond scum, lose their electrical footing. The miracle of walking on translucency has broken down.

I've got a small, pocket-sized dosimeter, I keep it on me at all times now. I'm holding it in my hand, checking the area around here. And even before I'm touched, I know what that stretched-out hand is planning to do.

She searches for my lips with hers, she presses down on my chest, which is heated up from running, from the search for Control Point 6. She probably wants to save me, to correct, if possible, her father's mistake. But it's not a question of a mistake, don't you get it?—there's no point in telling her this.

I now control the world, for a moment I've received the power that otherwise only birth and death bestow. All clocks have stopped, the drifting away of that childish love has stopped as well, the fading of her pale image. The agony ceases: of seeing her as always the same, of seeing her in the bright full-color comics of memory, frame by frame—how she slips out of your hands like a lifeline.

The dosimeter shudders in my hand. You lying old fart, I think. Liar and traitor—but whatever, live and let live. What's with this trial, these accusations—it's all bullshit, I don't blame anybody for anything. All you need are just a few such unique, exceptional moments, let the blows land, let the grasses sway, the sheets of rain, with me among them.

The great, the interesting, the notable—the miraculous, the fairytale—may they never fade away. May the sensors' arrows never quiet down, may iodine-131 continue to hang in the air amid the rain, a freeze-frame of magnetized droplets, may the half-life never end.

"Squeak-squeak"—like a little mouse with its toothy pliers cutting through the wires of a time bomb hidden in my groin—this is how the dosimeter starts to make noise. It lightly passes the indicator needle over the magnetic pad, crawling across the cliff—"squeak-squeak." Her hand slides across me, loaded like a weapon, to finish the unfinished business. I hope that finally the right moment will come, at least before we definitively and fatally harm ourselves.

My head is buzzing. It's like my brain itself is growing. This is it, radiation sickness, I tell myself.

Her hand searches for a way through my pants, under my T-shirt, toward my stomach, but the flag is wound around my waist, the color of blood, with a crest in the corner.

"Don't touch it!" yells the Pioneer on guard, the small sentry at the door to the dangerous void.

Now I have to stop, right here. I snatch up the bottle with the diagonal blue label *Ethyl chloride* and press down on the nozzle. A cold stream flows across my stomach. Then the freezing follows. "Me, too . . . spray me, too!" she whispers, her voice like embers. I turn my back to her, hiding the toy.

"No!"

"I want some, too!"

How beautiful she is, with wet hair stuck to her cheeks, her eyes deeper than ever. She knows what I've seen in them and immediately takes advantage of this, quickly repeating:

"I want some, too!"

Sometimes hitting or kissing is absolutely one and the same thing. But I don't do it. It's simply that I'm already numb, with winter skin, impervious to influence.

>>>

Now, after everything, she seems impossibly young, babyish, and this is the only thing that stops me—the infantile memory awakened by the invisible shaved hairs crushes me into dust, melts me, I release my grip. This probably disappoints her, the pain drains out of her body. But she also realizes: it's better to stop, better for both of us.

The clutching at each other ceases, falls away with a creak, she releases me from the bite of her grip and I remove my fingers from the wounds I had thrust my fingernails into. Blood quickly seals up the emptiness. The blue flesh of my elongated body emerges from conquered orifices. I fall onto my back, she drops onto one side, water flows out of both of us, through both of us.

Do I love her or hate her? No one has ever asked me anything more relative.

I hope that finally the right moment will come. The moment when we split up, the moment before the moment in which we definitively and in all seriousness really could harm ourselves.

I know there are theories that radiation striking the earth from the cosmos plays an important evolutionary role. Radiation, arriving from galaxies, in pulsars and quasars, exploding supernovas. A magic wand in the hand of God, with which He creates the *primordial state*.

In our original and final pose, we are always naked.

>>>

There's a sober-minded square inside me who puts up barriers—I hate him. He is what hinders me. He binds me with the hemp noose of the rope makers who unwound their wares along the endless Reeperbahn. I take empty steps, while in front of me something is waiting. Something and someone, the stuff of nightmares—but I wonder whether it isn't the stuff of perfect images as well? Such as prostitutes in tracksuits. Plain and simple, but I like their smiles:

"*Komm schon, Blondy!*"

"Komm schon, wir machen es atomisch!"

There's a very small room where the sober-minded square has peevishly entrenched himself. He stuffs wet towels under the door and breathes through a gasmask, he slips a hopcalite aspirator over the anteater-like snout. However, even this last bastion of resistance will fall. He deserves to meet the other in me. And the other in me deserves it, too.

My numb legs and feet in their crude shoes pound the banks along an arm of the Elba. The running continues.

Attempts to Replace the Comsomol with Sports
The running, the transformation into pain, doesn't lead me any farther from or closer to the goal, for now. But it's the only effective reality I have at my disposal.

The only thing I knew about adults was that adults, unlike children, go to work. But I didn't get what this meant.

Parents worked, neighbors did, too. The day was divided into work time and free time, with a lunch break and the hygienic half-day off, into the five-day work week plus that disputed slice of Saturday.

I took me a lot of time to grow up. It took me even more time to figure out what the point of that everyday motion was: so mechanistic and ingrained that it even turned vacations into work. An activity with regulated parameters, innocent and naïve, just like those men and women with their rounded shoulders who went to their offices every morning as if going on vacation.

I couldn't read yet. The only understandable things in the newspaper for me were the red splotches of the medals—the only colored elements, placed next to the masthead and surrounded with wreaths. I saw the determined profiles of nameless men—I had never seen in adults anything like the movement in those slanted brows, the tension captured in the portrait, as if caught mid-jump. Most adults tended toward chubbiness and on top of that often, even regularly, got sick. Pharmacies were a favorite meeting place, while the delivery of imported medicines for myriad and ever-more-threatening illnesses was a sign of elevated social status.

The newspapers watched me with their portraits, but then perhaps it was still too early to look for K-shev's face in the line-up. And perhaps it was still too early for him to step so far forward, to appear on the front page.

The newspapers showed traces of sausage and other cold cuts, along with dried tomato seeds, sometimes a spot of mustard, after the workers or clerks had finished their lunch break. There were brick-layers in paper hats, on which you could read the major headlines. The white village eggs, which were something entirely different, with their milky hue, arrived wrapped in small torn-up squares of newspaper.

I couldn't wait to grow up and be able to read: then I'd be able to understand the messages everyone else failed to notice, even though they were broadcast with such fat, black-scented letters. Or worse yet, they purposely pretended not to see them.

Instead, the adults became even heavier, they drooped, they began dragging their exhausted legs—surely from the pointless-ness of it all. I never figured it out in any case, and in my failure to understand I simply despised them. I begged them to sign me up for more and more new sports, and to leave me to my own devices. I strained my sinews, but despite this effort I didn't feel like I had achieved anything. "Bravo," they told me, "you're improving your-self." But I knew: if I continue on like this, I'll just end up as an average athlete, most probably a gym teacher. Then I joined the army. Then I was discharged. In the interim between these two events nothing happened. Nothing except getting close to K-shev from a rather strange angle, getting dangerously close alongside him and dangerously near.

>>>

Was I hoping for something more? Of course. My secret weapon was *Hope*—one of the socialist-era concrete jungles on Sofia's outskirts. By the way, I always knew that a white rabbit could pop out of the concrete top-hat of that neighborhood and cut across my life with joyful hops. Not expecting anything in particular doesn't mean that you don't have hopes. So I wasn't waiting for anything, on the contrary, I had even thoroughly given myself over to the general despair. And then it happened all of its own accord. I just had to get far enough away from home, to find myself in no-man's-land. What better place than the Hope neighborhood?

Late one evening I went into a store, the only one I would find open from here to downtown. I could feel my stomach growling, my head was practically spinning. But I didn't even ask myself why I was so hungry.

I bought bread and canned meat, chocolate and generic beer. Between the metal grating of the bread rack I saw a girl in a jean jacket near the alcohol display. Short, light-brown hair, curly. Her face made me stop and stare. She was about four or five meters away, she didn't see me. I was struck by how clean her skin seemed, if that means anything from such a distance, under the whitish sheen of the fluorescent lights. She seemed somehow self-assured, a badass. I wasn't surprised when I saw her head toward the checkout with a bottle of vodka. I hurried over there, too—not that I had anything in mind, I simply didn't want to let her out of my sight. So I could see her face, I got into the other checkout line. However, my line moved faster, so I went outside.

I leaned against the empty crates and broke off a hunk of bread. I started chewing, but that just made my stomach hurt even more. I sat down on a crate and leaned against the wall, I didn't care if I got dirty. I thought it would be best to catch a cab and go home.

The door opened and I saw her coming down the stairs. She wound the plastic bag around her hand and spit the gum out of her mouth.

Then something almost unbelievable happened: the spit-out gum somehow swerved and spun, it flew up and before I could duck, it hit me in the face, right on the cheek. She burst out laughing with her hand over her mouth. Then she stepped toward me and leaned over:

"Sorry!"

I lifted my hand, touched my cheek—I could feel the moist trace of her spit on my skin.

"I didn't mean to," she said, her gaze guilty, but not overly so. As if she were waiting for a cue from me to smile.

"Don't worry about it," I said. "No harm done." I put the bread back in the bag and stood up.

She then suggested taking me to some party, that's where she was headed. It was nearby, at her friend's. She showed me the bottle.

She had no reason to be worried, because I was already smiling back at her. For a split second I thought: had she noticed that I'd been watching her in the store? Then I just looked into her eyes—bluish, with long lashes.

So I agreed to go, even though it was out of character for me: an unknown neighborhood, a strange evening, somehow gloomy and desolate. Or maybe precisely because of that.

>>>
She struck me as a rather ordinary and not particularly interesting girl, at least at first glance. I'm sure if the whole thing hadn't been so ordinary, I never would have gone with her. What could we talk about, what could I expect from a girl in jeans who buys vodka and spits out her gum on the street? And what talking in any case—I preferred staying silent, especially after the army. There I'd learned the skill of shutting up instantly and staying that way for days. Just like during those endless rounds, alone on patrol in the heat, in the dead calm among the poplars. Everything repeated day after day, or every other day, it doesn't matter. The drills lose meaning and value—endless weeks of summer sentry duty, the ranks thin out, the shifts get longer. You get the feeling that in the end you'll be the only one left on the whole base—the buildings and barracks are empty, the armories are jam-packed with black machine guns like ancient bones, but besides the skeletons there's no one around. What is there to talk about, who is there to talk to?

I came back with that habit and it was convenient, I carefully preserved it until times changed. In the dark days of pointlessness, on those cold winter evenings without electricity, among people whose faces seemed smeared with ashes, scowling and wrinkled. People whose gazes were not so much despairing as devoid of any active thought—my silence was in harmony with that inert world fixated on itself. Just some phrase here and there, a single word said on the street, when passing a stranger's silhouette on the stairs.

Now, when I'm running and again silent, when the whistling of air in my lungs resembles a sharp internal shout meant to further inspire me. Now I'd like to know: what exactly I was thinking about during that time, during all those mute months and years? I can't have forgotten, that's impossible. It would be terrible to think that I was waiting only for that: getting out, the elementary freedom of movement, and, of course—communication with girls' bodies, which is the only thing that saves you from the need to be constantly moving, running, patrolling your post all night. Otherwise you'll have to wallow in forgetfulness and nonchalance like all the others, to fatten up. The youths with whom only a year ago I had first stood at attention had changed, they were no longer boys, which meant they had filled out—with thickened necks, rounded out with flab—even when they were fairly muscular. Even when they were healthy village boys used to physical labor, boys for whom—unlike us urbanites—physical strength was a natural condition instead of scrawniness, weakness, the inexplicable infirmity of glasses perched on one's nose. They all grew heavy, weighing down their own bodies, and began dragging their feet in exhaustion. Was it the pointlessness that was poisoning them—did they do it to spite the army, stubbornly withholding the gift of their fresh physique? There wasn't much point for such a physique to exist here anyway, arrested in inactivity. Just as I felt I was being wasted, unneeded. I deserved other epaulettes, other clothing, I knew which ones.

It would've been naïve and embarrassing to say it aloud, but I hadn't forgotten my childish-youthful goals, I still remembered the paragliders, the taste of my dreams of being a parachutist, we wanted to be paratroopers, and those wings, crossed on Gagarin's emblems and epaulettes.

I remained proud. My contempt for the niggling dreams of my fellow soldiers was not a reason to claim, however, that dreams didn't exist at all. The only thing was—I didn't understand which ones, I failed to look into it. I didn't ask anyone—like I said, I was pretty much silent. The rest of the time I spent working out and being the model soldier. You've never seen anything like it.

Of course, swallowing back tears and clenching my teeth behind whitened lips, I had to fight for every ounce of muscle mass. For every fiber I wove into the elastic bands that rolled and unrolled my joints. Could I really have been so naïve? What thoughts worried me, how I clenched the bar between my fingers to bruising, doing pull-ups: fifty, fifty-one, fifty-two, I didn't stop until my tendons froze up, with a pain in my ribs and chest, until my elbows stretched out with a creak as if falling apart. But how else could I guarantee my upward path? How exemplary a Pioneer, Comsomol member, soldier, private, corporal and so on did I have to be, I asked myself, in order to finally become the Third Bulgarian Cosmonaut? I didn't know the secret pathways to this starry career, but I could at least take care of the physical preparation on my own. Even there in the rack for beating carpets in the courtyard or on the bar made of welded pipes between the whitewashed curbstones on the base's parade grounds—in my sleep, even, I voluntarily tormented my limbs and stomach muscles with new and heavier weights. The feeling is so strong—the physical sensation, that is—that I want to stop the moment, that moment, that hanging with strained arms. As if balancing on the blade of the body, turned into a drill, as I lower myself down over her belly. And not only to stop these movements with the egotistical goal of remaining within them infinitely, but also to succeed in stopping the very movement beyond them, toward infinity. And to stop the memories. This hasn't happened to me with any other girl, *only with her*—she erases all memories in her wake and they cease to exist to a certain extent. And I cease to exist to a certain extent. That's it, perhaps that's why I want to stop that moment in time, to stop time itself.

I was envious of the healthy, solid skeletons upon which the bodies of my fellow pawns in the army seemed to be built. Dressed so naturally in their skin, and the skin itself so naturally colored, impervious to the influences of the atmosphere. Their skin was somehow differently pigmented, since it didn't get so bitterly and painfully ruined as mine did at the very first attempt to look the sun straight in the eye. So what cosmos for me in that case?, you may ask. Never mind that the government itself had already given up on its space program.

Yes, you're right. The thing is, however, that even after the army I continued—albeit in some kind of mourning—to search for the absolute. But why along such ridiculous paths? I don't know, but I simply agreed and the two of us—the girl with the vodka—set off.

>>>

We set off through the apartment blocks. It's close, she said, and went on talking. I was carrying the rather heavy bag with the tin can, bread, and beer. I was expecting it to break any minute, that's why I was clutching it. So I would look even more ridiculous.

For at least a short while I didn't feel hungry. But I didn't even ask myself that question—why am I so hungry all the time?! My only thoughts were: maybe I should take off, go home, open up the can. And eat it with toasted bread, drink the beer, and sit down with the chocolate as desert in front of the television, if there's anything good on. But we passed by the bus stop, I kept walking with her. I would have to walk home, I didn't know how far it was back downtown. Hopefully this party would be worth it—although I had my doubts.

I'm talking about the time when 24-hour stores could be counted on one hand and nobody had even heard of a Chinese restaurant.

I'm talking about the time when I was twenty.

>>>

It was a narrow living room in a panel-block apartment, an apartment block in the midst of all the other apartment blocks. There were two guys about my age sitting there. One of them was probably the friend she'd mentioned to me and the other guy was his friend. There were no girls there and—I would suspect—there had never been any. On the low press-board table stood an empty wine bottle and a half-full bottle of liquor, one of those completely undrinkable kinds. The new bottle didn't seem to pique as much interest as my arrival, but even that lasted only briefly. At least they acted like they didn't care and left the questions for later. They poured vodka into their glasses and left her standing. They didn't ask her about me, she'd brought me here and that was that, without "why" or "how." Maybe the only girl in the group enjoyed special privileges. Then the question logically arose: why was she the one sent to buy alcohol at 11 P.M.? The answer: so as not to risk being recognized at the store, the very same store where earlier they had stolen the wine and liquor. That explained the strange choice of drinks, since these dusty bottles were always on the very back shelf in the corner, where no one ever passes by, so it's a cinch to hide them under your shirt.

"Pour him a drink, why don't you!" she shouted from time to time, pointing at me. "Don't be a tight-ass, I bought the vodka. And I spit on him to boot, the poor guy."

It was the sad, gloomy, and impoverished time of the Transition, without electricity.

It was a convenient time for the illusion that the Comsomol and all the memories that went along with it could be finished off once and for all. The past, which is eminently accusable, even though it can no longer repay you with anything.

When you see a million and a half neatly tucked in a briefcase on the table, those illusions capsize like canoes and the truth gapes in front of you. For all your moral causes, for all your unfulfilled dreams you haven't gotten a single penny. No matter how righteous your cause, *that guy*, K-shev, for example, still managed to collect the dividend, despite his wrongness, despite the brazenness of his crime. Somehow he cashed in your very self.

>>>

Running makes me all the more hostile—if that's even possible. I know what's going to happen after another kilometer if I don't stop or slow down. It's not necessary for me to do one or the other—my body is now moving on its own, the running is automatic, as mechanical as it is unpleasant, single-minded, surrendering to the pain that keeps growing in every muscle and especially the joints. And I myself have already noticed that I'm trying to do something that's perhaps out of line, deceitful. To force a whole swath of my past through the fleshy filter that is the body. To burn it up as if in a stove, to cremate it by doing exercises to fill the emptiness inside me. I've done this before, I thought I'd given it up—but what do you know, when backed into a corner I run again toward it like the only escape route. Replacing the unfinished gestures of the past with active athletic movements—it's absurd, boring, pitiful. And just look how many more runners there are here around me. The Germans, and particularly those from Hamburg, probably yearn for some impossible part of the gestures from the past. Or they just want to be healthy.

>>>

The time of the Transition, like I said. The attempts to replace the Comsomol with athletics had no way of achieving a total effect, despite superficial successes. The army also didn't offer me anything more than a familiar backdrop. Distorted features of an image impressed upon me by youthful romanticism. Formerly handsome and monolithic, it would now look me in the eye polluted, with scratches on its very pupils. After being discharged I felt more confused about myself than ever.

Later—I'm talking about the time when the Transition was over and nothing external could be altered—in yet another attempt to change my very self, I resorted to my usual method. When I decided to take up boxing, however, I had no idea that my nose would get broken so quickly. Knowing my own character, I was afraid that after two or three workouts at the gym my self-confidence would skyrocket and I'd be unable to control myself, I'd bait somebody on the street and get my ass kicked. But let me reiterate that I'm talking about the time when violence had already taken on a new meaning. Just like the street itself, by the way. Collective spaces had shrunk, the street was the line of demarcation. And I always felt one category lighter than necessary, a slightly lower weight-class than everyone else. Who knows, maybe that was the reason I chose boxing—in the hopes that speed would compensate for mass. I also think that the incident from that night made a difference.

But things turned out differently than I expected. My nose was broken not in the outside world, but in the gym, at the second practice session. It wasn't even during sparring, they wouldn't let me get anywhere near the ring yet. It's a mistake to think that the padded helmet that protects your cheekbones and chin will also protect your nose if you yourself aren't protecting it. They smacked me good and despite the fact that the gloves soften the blow to some extent, I felt such a strong and blunt pain that with no qualms whatsoever I immediately felt like bawling, which I did. With tears, but silently. My coach wasn't moved, he just stuffed wads of cotton up my nose and said that that was the beginning.

I decided, however, that it was the end and went into the locker room to gather up my stuff. Tears, like I said, have a strange, contradictory power.

I didn't become a real street boxer. Even after tireless exercises targeting specific aspects of my body and mind, a fair amount of my original inconsistency still existed. Passivity, mixed with surprising and unexpected outbursts of hidden rage. Presumably the Party, just like the Comsomol before it, had no use for such quickly detonating fireworks. Plodding mediocrity is preferred, since it is far more predictable and can be governed. This must've been the reason that the Comsomol spurned me, in a sense that it spurned all of us together, following the example of the Party itself—like a fossilized creature giving a final croak beneath its shell and going belly up. We had become too spontaneous, the freedom of our bodies turned order into chaos.

>>>

Everything happened very quickly, during that night, I mean. The guy, the tall one whose bulging Adam's apple was somehow ugly and menacing—he cracked first, his gaze became hostile, dangerous, and I felt the threat. At such moments it's as if I'm seized by a strange sense of weightlessness.

She was sitting by me on the armrest of the battered sofa, holding onto my shoulder. She was touching me somehow ambiguously, but every time that guy, the tall one, tried to grab her around the waist, she would pull away, turning her back on him.

"Hey, whore," that's all he said, but it sounded sufficiently frightening.

"What are you playin' at?" I saw the other guy snarl, emboldened. He was short and unpleasant in his track suit.

I didn't realize the three of them had known each other for such a short time. It only now became clear to me—this was some kind of random boozing or hoodlum hang-out, they'd gotten together, found each other that night. What had I gotten myself into? The question crossed my mind. I had to run, to get out of there. I got up abruptly—why? To run for the door? I don't know, I stood up.

"As for you, douchebag," the tall one snarled and took a swing.

I could've stepped back, for example, because the movement of his arm was drunken and unsteady and way too slow. I didn't move, though, I didn't step back; his fist just got heavier from the slow swing and managed to take aim, connecting with my cheekbone and partially with the nose.

Good thing I didn't yell—that somehow startled them, because I didn't even raise a hand to my face, I just shut my eyes for a moment. When I opened them and looked around again, I saw that they were staring at me rather strangely.

"This is the force of nonresistance to force," I thought to myself. "Like Mahatma Gandhi."

Okay, so I didn't think it *then*, but now when I remember it, I think it.

And then she started shouting, baring her teeth, her voice unexpectedly loud and sharp, husky from cigarettes:

"You dirty bastards! I knew you'd do it! Who you think you are, huh, who?" She barely came up to the tall guy's shoulder, and leaning forward like that she looked even smaller, but somehow, I'm certain, it didn't matter to her anymore. "Do you think you'd found yourself some stupid bimbo? You know what my name is?

Do you? Do you know what's gonna happen now? Do you know who my father is?!"

All of a sudden a passport appeared in her hand—from back in the day, those green passports with the black-and-white photo and the coat of arms, you know the ones—and she was waving it around. She even smacked him on the nose with it, whacked him in the face as if he were some little twerp. And he was ripped, like I said. At that moment, neither she alone nor the two of us together could've done anything to fight them off, we didn't have a chance. But she slapped him across the face and laughed, kind of brattily, demonstratively, taking pleasure in humiliating him—that was what really did the trick, I figure. That's what it seemed like to me at that moment, although I couldn't really understand what was going on. Maybe I'd been KO'd.

K-shev, as he is understood, is a construct, the product of some moment or other of need or threat. In fact, you could say that he's even ready-made, since part of him has to be thought up, while the other part of him exists in any case: somewhere *up there*, somewhere invisible. Some K-shev or other was nevertheless real.

And they were freaked out, they jumped when they heard his last name—without even looking at the name in the passport. And since they were drunk on top of everything, it scared the shit right out of them.

>>>

We ran between the apartment blocks, then across the bridge toward the train station. We were laughing, and she kept asking: "Did he hit you hard?"

No, not really, I would answer, despite the fact that my teeth were numb. Such a night, of course, is unforgettable. I got home—without the bag of food, as it turned out—but with her instead. I wasn't hungry anymore. We shut the doors and windows tight, turned out the lights, and the music, cranked up to ten, exploded in our heads.

>>>

I, of course, am deeply convinced that the world revolves around me—as its center or at least as the object of its dictatorship. The idea is grandiose and never gets tiresome. Until you finally decide to enter real life.

Like a needle jabbed into your arm, reality stings you, hurting more than your skin and flesh. You realize that you're nobody. The electricity's gone out, the darkness is your sudden enemy—an ally and enemy simultaneously because it demands action—you have to protect yourself from the dark. Otherwise the world goes out, along with the artificial light from the power plant. The night once again disintegrates into atoms, changes from cultivated to wild, fitting itself afterward into its original black hues, its cat skin.

Too bad if you find yourself lying on the carpet with your pants down when the lights come back on. With a sticky stain on your stomach—a pathetic wanker.

Such nights, like the night after my escape with Hope from Hope, compensates for all my patheticness for months on end. In the morning, however, she left, which was to be expected. She didn't like the decor. She liked me, as she said, more than she should have. So it wouldn't be cool to steal my cash or some valuables from the closet. For that reason she decided upfront, *like an honest dude*, as she put it—to take off. What kind of dude are you, I asked her, which was also an excuse to touch the crotch of her jeans. I smiled, hoping she'd let me strip her again, even if it was only at the door, a goodbye quickie, standing there like that with my bare feet on the tile. But no.

This girl hadn't been *that* girl. In the morning I secretly snuck a peek—I'll admit it—at her passport. Her name wasn't K-sheva, of course, but then again I didn't expect it to be. Her last name started with G.

Yet I had somehow believed in the myth *of the father*. And that thought, as it turns out, never left me. My obsession with predestination was obviously entering a new phase.

>>>

I don't think I'm an exception. Everyone my age—how many times have they experienced humiliation, how many times have they come face-to-face with violence, so innocently hidden in the ridiculous outbursts of demonic childhood? The pockets shaken down in school, the stolen small change, the backpack scattered on the ground. The ball popped and skewered on the metal spikes of the fence. These dregs are washed away with time, especially when you pass through the key moment when you yourself can and indeed must—inevitably—commit violence.

But I remember, I've etched it in my brain, I can't shake it off, I can't smile, I can't get free of it. The cyclical motion in which you change from victim to perpetrator, those gears keep slipping for me. Time doesn't turn its spokes. The circle of nature that torments or delights you, depending on your participation and role—it all seems senseless to me. Where is it leading, what's its cause, its reason? What should I hope for, why should I pay a high price since I'll fail to remember its value, I'll forget it.

I don't want to forgive, I can't forgive. The time taken from me cannot be returned. What if those moments, even those filled with suffering—like that punch in the face years ago—had no meaning? What will happen then with the night after that instant of humiliation, after that second of fear in the crumbling panel block-apartment with its flickering, naked light bulbs? The price of the night with the girl from Hope and my reckless inspiration with her dark, almost black body in the gloom—wouldn't it, too, be diminished, if the ordeal is diminished? No, I don't want to, I can't forget.

>>>

The Comsomol could not easily be replaced. I tried sports, I tried other religions. I counted on the army with particular enthusiasm: I was supposed to become a pilot after all! I only later discovered the reason for this attraction, when the dream was already dead.

I'm a good runner and thus I became not a pilot, but a foot soldier.

Every boy dreams of becoming a cosmonaut, but then he takes up something easier: girls. After that, or more or less at the same time, he starts to smoke, although at the beginning, of course, he coughs. Later it becomes clear—you really have to be a complete geek to not replace the cosmonaut with something more realistic. Okay, so I was stuck in that phase for a long time. I remember our classes in Morals and Law in school and the basketball-esque physique of our teacher, a philosopher, six-and-a-half feet tall.

"So, in your opinion," he asked me pleasantly, although I think he felt like smacking me upside the head, but at the time I didn't understand why, "what's the path of evolution, of development? After a just society has been created and all needs have been met—what's next?"

"After that," I answered after thinking it over a bit, "man will turn toward the cosmos. He'll conquer the space beyond the earth."

"Aha," my comrade teacher nodded knowingly. And he didn't hit me.

But he should've. I needed to learn at least something in school, even at the price of violence, because there's no way to save ourselves from violence, it catches up with us sooner or later.

I would go home, take off my backpack, toss it down and separate the one outside from the one inside. I would fall asleep. The nights didn't have any connection to the days. There were cats wailing in the courtyards like children. The outrageous ecstasies of nocturnal love. I didn't understand it then, but the consciousness also processed that information, unthinkingly. And that's how I began to suspect that night was the time for battles, for struggles. But who was the enemy?

Quite early—that's what I'm trying to say—painful shadows crept over love. Does that make more sense?

That "who is the enemy" always eluded me. The question wasn't satisfied with the answers from war games; besides, girls weren't allowed to play anyway. Only concrete, real death—without games, without roles that you can step out of—death alone eased at least a little of the emptiness that we would now call "the ideological model." With childish cruelty we doggedly attacked the ants crawling between the rocks. We barraged their columns with bombs of hot plastic as they scrambled, panicked, into pockets in the ground. Falling, hissing globs that melted into black smoke. Crawling black tears from the mouth of an empty Vero detergent bottle with its top set on fire . . .

Yes, I had my reasons for looking forward to the army. But it was precisely because of these optimistic hopes that the idiocy of it hit me so hard and, in the end, became yet another disappointment.

The Army, Infantry

Everything began with mild attempts: how much can you handle? Individual training tests the foundations of the psyche, which will be necessary later on—the system had made secret calculations about my career. The system itself had already failed, but I personally had been given a head start, acceleration. Is it worth forgetting the lessons learned during those three months of quiet September hell, infantry battalion? The system now has reason to be scared—I don't forget easily. Like a pin-drum in the music box of my heart, through the holes in the aortas, some goal was filtering its signal, the music of the hollow barrel-organ was playing its commands.

I'm not trying to say, Comrade Commander-in-Chief, that two hours of unenlightened marching are some kind of limit. I'm not trying to say that two mandatory years of service, Comrade Commander-in-Chief, just two of the impressionable and golden years of my youth, are reason to try to settle the score at the price of such cruel diligence. But the rage within me, my dear comrade, even then had something else in mind. I have to admit I regret that I didn't believe it—back then, at the time.

Because at quite a young age—at a perversely and criminally young age—I met her. Comrade Commander-in-Chief, there are things that go beyond the barrier of military secrets. Things that make the memory rather specific, and for that reason I'm only able to share them with you personally. Of course, I'll also share the physical gesture of my repentance as well. You see, it's for that reason that I run so selflessly, to make it on time. By the way, in the infantry no one taught us how we should run—and that's strange, don't you think? No characteristic features of leaping advances across flat terrain, to say nothing of rugged country. Why was running somehow taken for granted in and of itself: *Am I born to run, perhaps?* But I'm impoverished ideologically, comrade, and for that reason to this very day, I don't know whether I'm running properly. I suspect not. I run quickly, I run recklessly, energetically, but my bones fuse from the effort, my joints creak, you can already hear them, because I'm inevitably getting closer to you, to the new location of your temporary headquarters, Mr. Commander-in-Chief—your white hospital. I was left to learn everything on my own—at least I liked running. The drills, however, the marching, shackled me in the chains of their exercises more and more, with the soured sweetness of torture. Like a merry-go-round, an endless spiral of broken ellipses, in a circle, left and right, the legs intermingling.

And still, I would obey every fitting command that would allow me to make my way to K-shev more quickly and directly, even if this way pierces deeply into death itself. My running is ugly, but somehow effective, I sense the rhythm. However, I found marching in a closed column unbearable, the brink of madness—doing something orderly, yet devoid of meaning. Marching is an art, the Comrade Sergeant was always saying: finding ourselves in the museum itself, we stumbled along to obliviousness on the exhibits that were our feet.

How and when did we give someone else the right to command us like mechanical toys, right down to the smallest movements of our arms and legs, fastened with bolts at the joints? Every moment when a hand reached out, deliberately slow, to give us a foretaste and for it to get a foretaste of the degradation—time would stop. When you could no longer take the standing, not out of exhaustion and not out of tension, but because of the helplessness, because of the senselessness. The horizon that has bitten into your own time like a toothless mouth. Time hasn't even stopped—you simply realize now that it was never really passing.

Childhood, those naïve lessons at school, were an illusion that life is valuable in and of itself. The army is that blessed experiment that divides the body on the one hand from its meaning on the other. In the sun, in a uniform sewn with an unimaginable flair for discomfort. In scratchy fabric that even wild tribes wouldn't wrap their dead in before tossing them into the grave—there and as such, here and now you stand. And while the sun crawls slowly overhead, as if waiting for you to curse it, insulting comparisons explode in the brain. Curses and insults want to fly off your tongue toward your very self—but why?

Yes, the sun, you tell yourself, is crawling terribly slowly. *Like shit.* You spit the filth out of your mouth, but you've already gulped it down, you're already cursing, already swearing every other word like all the others. Who do you dislike and who do you hate now? With stripes also comes the right for you to commit abuses—"I can't! I won't!"—but you do it. You do it with relish, nasty and slow. Some frustrated sergeant, some I, hardboiled from boredom.

The sun, contrary to all expectations, shines on everyone with equal indifference and your problem is not solved. You're no longer innocent, you've lost the right and the moral assets of victimhood. You sense it, that fiery glob of brains, its sadistic immobility. It sounds impossible, the maddening thought that the projector's yellow light has to make at least 700 more circles at that same lazy pace before two years will be over, the brain is incapable of comprehending this. And the future, which is actually the truth, is transformed into fiction. And until then, consequently, you are simply nobody.

I've counted the minutes, I've counted the seconds, strung taut at my post by the flag, every second thinking up the name of a girl, known or unknown, but please, I beg you, let her be a runner, please make her legs speed up the clock hands at least a little! At the most banal moment in my life I sense the very depths of the ineptness—and at the same time the talent—of that devil who created the system. It's as moronically simple as Chinese water torture, as that staff idiot who purposely keeps the door to his office, which reeks of linoleum and cigarette ashes, open. You expect him to peek out at any second, you know he's lurking, just so you can't figure out a way to get some relief. The pulsating, repetitive thought: there's no way to put down your weapon, it's impossible even to glance at the clock, there's no way out, didn't I tell you? Moments in which you offer a year of life in exchange for a half-hour less of this un-life. Moments that you will pass over with a smile years later. But not me, I tell myself—not me. I remember. I hate. I despise.

> *No matter how many*
> *years will pass by*
> *I won't resign myself*
> *to that—*
> *we don't want to relive*
> *unlived things!*

Like everyone else, my favorite band at the time was The Crickets, too.

1989
Blind time, as if jerking awake after dozing off unexpectedly.

"I'm not a Communist!" I yell in my sleep, lathered in sweat. I stand up: "And I never will be!"

Otherwise they wouldn't let me into the demonstrations.

Demonstrations

There were plenty of girls at the demonstrations. All quivering with excitement, I'd say. This is how I'd describe them: quivering with excitement and ultra-sensitive. I wonder whether *she* wasn't there among them? But how would I recognize her without an exploratory grope? No, I hadn't fallen so low as to sheepishly rub up against their bodies—I walked straight ahead with my head held high, chanting the necessary slogans, while I let that same old anger blaze in my eyes, something you still can't quite fully achieve. Regardless of whether the elections were won, the thirst remains—the girls of democracy were especially impressed by this seemingly magical gaze. But I walked right on through them, I hardly noticed them, I was looking for something different, I wanted all of them together, at the same time, yet because of my clear recognition that it could never happen, I was looking for something that would bring it all together—the body of one girl who was different. Like being amid the trees in a wet forest, orienteering between bodies, among so many women with feverish skin, which is twice as sensitive.

Under those circumstances there was no way to avoid a spark blazing up in a more general sense. Amid so many suppressed desires, the flaring up of sparks is imperative. It heightens the sensation of an explosion, of expanding space in which insignificant bodily processes take on the scope of atmospheric phenomena. Collective energy should not be underestimated, but who can control it? Certainly not me.

And to rub our noses in it—that is, in short, as intimidation—K-shev and his people, quite experienced in Party-style electrical engineering, harnessed the thunder and lightning hanging over the ruins of the Party structure. They stripped the lightning rods of their precious metals and left the negative waves to be unleashed in a controlled burn, for their own good and for the satisfaction of the general public.

I was there in order to understand, as it were, that an inescapable logic controls my fate. For that reason, the wee hours of August 27th in front of the burning Party Headquarters also have a deeper meaning for me. And it is not symbolic, not merely symbolic as for everyone else.

What I remember most of all is this: it smelled terrible. Be it from the hissing panels in the hallways, from the droplets of aging tar mixed with decades-old dust that came sizzling out through the holes, burned away by red hot nails. Or from the melting sausage in the burning storerooms on the ground floor. And on top of everything—the scent of boiling Freon erupting through the cylinders of charred refrigerators—it smelled terrible, that much I remember.

>>>

I think that even there, at that very place, I ritually sacrificed part of myself—the fire was sufficiently strong to warm my blood to the decision. The red neckerchief blazed up and transformed into a black fuse even before the flames lapped at it. It immediately reminded me of the dripping streams of ash from the lit-up bottle of Vero dish soap. The cloth burned up instantly, without a trace. So did the shirt with the bleached collar. But first I tore the Bulgarian Communist Youth League emblem off the front of it. It was a nice shirt, I thought to myself—it fit me well. At the ends of its short sleeves there was a rather wide, turned up cuff. I don't know why, but as I destroyed the wardrobe of the past, I heard engines and trains going by, chaotic noises, like the sound of a guerrilla propaganda movie unrolling its reels somewhere. Or was I just hearing things?

I know that K-shev himself also wanted to destroy something in that fire, otherwise he wouldn't have set it—but why? Just to obliterate some stupid old documents, traces? To sneak out the back door with the money along with the strongbox—just like he'd done before—while the suckers out front rushed in to save the wounded?

In that sense, running toward a confrontation with him, I'm not looking for confessions or apologies. And that's precisely why he's waiting for me. How much longer can those doctors continue to treat him? They'll only give up when the regular payments stop rolling in. It's very easy to switch off the IVs if that's what the patient's loved ones want. They need only to hint that the cost has become excessive. And, in fact, the cost is ridiculously high, especially for an old man like him . . .

. . . for a sick old man like me.

>>>

For ten years the party paid for my treatment, for the next five—the remnants of the old upper echelon, my fellow antiques, with long years of service to the party under their belts. For some time I was still necessary to various circles, which vied with each other to pay for my salvation. However, when symbols become devoid of meaning, they must be recast. After the fifteenth year it became clear that I only caused them trouble. They've washed their hands of me and my demise is simply a matter of time. I know, I know all too well: you have to leave the wounded to die of their wounds. In that pouring rain—I remember well, there, as we were retreating through the forest—there, through the half-open door of the church, next to the monastery, I overheard just that: "leave the dead to bury their dead." Now that's what gave me the courage.

Out of the five partisans from our detachment who had managed to stay half alive, four of them fell on the road through the gorge. Two were killed or at least fatally wounded, I saw it with my own eyes. My comrade whose guerrilla name was Chavdar got stuck in the swamp—he couldn't crawl out along the fallen tree because his leg was injured. I'm sure I should've tried to help him, I should've gone back down, broken off the branches, pulled him out. I should've stripped down and tied my shirt and sweater into a rope. But I didn't, what would've been the point anyway? The police were sure to arrive any second, and catch me in the middle of my heroics. I turned my back on him and kept on climbing. Then I thought I heard a popping sound, as if I'd stepped on a dry branch, but I hadn't—I assume he shot himself in the mouth, but the mud of the swamp muffled the sound.

I saw the fourth one of the five of us running after me up the slope like a shadow. He was clutching a grenade in his right hand. It's really wet, I thought to myself, with all this rain the primer is never going to ignite, it's ridiculous. He didn't have any other weapon, so he kept clutching the grenade, even now, in desperation. If only I'd taken Comrade Chavdar's revolver. If only I'd been able to pull my revolutionary brother out of the swamp. But it was too late now, it didn't matter. Get rid of that grenade, I told him, put it away, we have to retreat. We have to retreat, I said, as if I were still commanding a detachment. As if there weren't only five of us left, and now only two out of the five. And a little baggage—a radio transmitter, a notebook full of watchwords, passwords, and codenames of go-betweens, all written on cigarette papers inside a tobacco case. Traitor, I think he said. Why, I don't know. Traitor, he repeated and squeezed the grenade in his mangled hand.

It's only now that I realize that this comrade most likely had a bent *for leftist fanaticism. I know that look: revolution to the bitter end, red terror. Actually, grenades are best suited to anarchists, for that reason our commissar, who knew all the recruits, didn't issue him his own weapon—untrustworthy. Even though the truth was that the kid didn't have any fingers on his hand—they'd been cut off during an interrogation at the police headquarters.*

But no matter, I'm not one for crying over such things. I hit him once, it was enough. His body slid down the rocky slope into the ravine and in an instant he was gone. It was over.

I'm left alone, so now I can ditch the radio transmitter; against my chest under my windbreaker is a leather pouch full of documents. And the little suitcase, the strongbox, of course, the revolution's gold reserves, the fruit of many years' labor. Money for the insurrectional revolutionary committee—money that was donated, or confiscated, voluntarily, or not quite. The suitcase was nice and full, our comrade commissar wasn't a spendthrift, not a single cent went to waste. Rightly so, comrade!—our comrade commissar, may he rest in peace, was the first to fall in the ambush.

Saturday, a requiem in the church. The voice of the priest and the cantor, singing deeply, as if in a well. Up above on the roof tiles, where the awning butts up against the monastery gates, drops are pelting down, the rain doesn't stop. My eyes are closing—in the oats, I tell myself, in the sacks of hay is the best hiding place. I can't let myself fall asleep, yet my eyes are closing on their own, I hear them whispering inside, with the cross, with the censer. The cantor is singing or reading something, undoubtedly from the Epistles. Then the priest: Leave, he says, the dead to bury their dead. Traitor, I say to myself, and fall asleep just like that. It's only then that I see the donkey—munching oats in silence, his back is wet, sticking out from under the overhang, the rain pouring down on him from above.

>>>

And there really was an office there, I saw it, ratty with a broken-down door, in the center of the hallway, in the center of the central wing, where with watering yet curious eyes I went down the smoke-filled corridors. In order to realize that it was burning *of its own accord*—the Party Headquarters, lit up like a Christmas tree from the tension of memory-laden holiday electricity. Self-ignition, self-immolation, intended to illuminate—or to make futile all illumination of—the interior of the secret.

And from deep inside I saw his skull—there really was a person there, either real or an actor. Some extra, an impostor, left to stroll in the lamplight, to throw shadows on the curtains, in the windows glowing in the night like eyes.

In the end the bonfire collapsed in on itself, the last dying spark of the five-pointed star fell into the ashes. In the morning, after nights like this one, there remains only cold, clumped dust, like black talcum powder on a photographic negative. And the sense of something unfinished.

The path to justice somehow turned out to be long and painful. Contempt grew during the long stretch before its realization—but not contempt for K-shev, but for all the others who delayed the decision. Rather deep contempt.

>>>

When I leave the stone atrium of the burning and hissing Party Headquarters, I find myself in the Empty Space, where just moments ago there had been a crowd in the mood for revolution. There were still people there—after all, I wasn't alone in rushing inside, weren't they rushing in right alongside me? But now I

come down the steps, look around with wide-open, sleepy eyes—
and there is no one on the yellow-paved square. No one.

That's what I really hate, their running away. K-shev didn't
run away anywhere, he didn't scamper off to save himself from
uncomfortable questions. He is not anonymous, in fact, he is the
focus. He really is a construct, yet his name still does the trick, as
a necessity or a threat.

And they got scared all right, they jumped right out of their
skins when he began to flare up—from the inside, from his idola-
trous, hollow womb. Because they didn't have any fire of their own
to fight him with, they turned their backs and hid in the darkened
streets, to avoid being melted down. Lugging stolen things—cups,
food, chairs and televisions, bottles of sunflower oil. Even in the
night's fake flames, reeking like burning rubber and gasoline, even
then some yellow suns managed to turn their wheels. The people
ran, saving themselves from the overwhelming heat. The sun was
shining from another place. The isolation of the darkness stretched
between it and the square, yet it was as if we suddenly sensed its
breathing. The other side of the sun. The dark side of things. It
gaped for a second and blinked like the eyelid of an unknown
colossus. So as not to process what they had seen, everyone simply
gasped. And since most of them were drunk on top of everything,
they simply swallowed their tongues.

I remember. I hate. I despise them. If I had the chance, I'd
punish them over and over again, every time with the same thing:
fear that transforms into horror. But I don't think even that would
be enough. Those two guys should have raped her in that crappy
apartment, without a second thought. They should've kicked my
ass—who knows, maybe even killed me. I should've burned up in
that building, released by someone like a rat into a maze, along

with all the rest of them. The firemen who kept not showing up. The victims who became perpetrators—without necessarily wanting to, without wanting to at all—simply out of curiosity. I don't remember very well: was I, too, carrying a blazing torch made of rolled-up Party newspapers? If they wanted to, they could probably convince me of it. For my part, I would admit it—not for their, but rather for my own personal, satisfaction. I would confirm every act of participation and non-participation, of aggression or passivity, with which or without which the revolution took place. Because the revolution itself is also a fabrication: there was no revolution. No change was brought about, K-shev simply changed his country. Meaning that he packed his bags to go on vacation, to go take a cure abroad. Now I am familiarizing myself visually with his destination—on the way to the clinic, running.

On the way to the clinic, in a sprint, which finally makes me vomit.

Vomiting

This is the fifteenth kilometer, the physical limit, the barrier. The stomach erupts, the diaphragm sucks air downward and purges everything. I didn't stop in time, I didn't cut short my sprint, maybe I even wanted it to happen like that, to fall to the pavement, trampled by the athletes who move through Hamburg's morning haze in deer-like bounds. But I don't fall, training is training, after all: my palms slam onto my thighs of their own accord for support, my kneecaps rasp over the joints. On the ground between my shoes—a splotch of stomach acid and wetness; sweat drips from my face. I haven't eaten since last night, there's the little dead ball of airplane food, swallowed up and tossed back out gain.

But I still can't breathe, the ellipses just outside my field of vision are still quavering. I've still got half a minute to go, within thirty seconds my ribcage should have recovered from its collapse. The muscles that expand and contract the ribs—let them come back into action. "Let breathing commence," commands the national sports medicine doctor, Comrade K-shev, who, despite being in a coma, continues to wait for me. And for that reason I don't want to faint here, ironically, on this path, which runs into the first street next to the coastal road and where a sign hangs right above my head:

A. S. MAKARENKO-STRASSE

Go to hell, Anton Semyonovich!

2

*

DEEDS & DOCUMENTS

Lexicon

of one boy's personal aversions to K-shev

1) He wasn't handsome, he didn't look like a good guy, not even like a bad guy—in short, he just wasn't handsome. He wasn't ugly, either. He didn't possess that certain something that inspires love/fear in the heart of a child.

2) He never smiled; instead, he snickered frequently.

3) He wasn't tall enough to be a giant. He wasn't short enough to be a dwarf.

4) He clucked his tongue like he was trying to remove something stuck between his teeth. What?

5) They say he loved pork and tripe and garlic. Why?

6a) He liked having people listen to him sing, but it was unbearable. He sang in the shower. His voice gurgled through the pipes.

6b) So why didn't he ever arrange for the repair of the drainage and sewer systems? The city reeks, especially during the summer.

7) He didn't send his daughter to the same school where they sent me.

8) He hid her from everyone.

9) ~~He beat her.~~

9) Maybe he did something else to her?

10) What?

\>\>\>

The first time we did it absolutely unintentionally.

We were driving through the foothills of the mountains. It was early, she was driving, I was flopped back on the passenger's seat, dozing. She drove steadily and beautifully, as always, and I drifted off. She was breathing quietly, almost noiselessly, there was only the noise of the motor. As if I were going down the road all by myself, savoring memories of the night.

Some sudden movement startled me, the car veered to the side. Then I saw the guardrail and the frozen stones wrapped in snow and spattered with mud. I saw a pile of gravel, quite close. With painful effort the windshield wipers dragged themselves to the right, trembling, then to the left, and in the cleaned-off embrasure we saw once more the gaping edge of the ravine. I saw her hands turning the wheel. We spun around once more and the wheels locked back into the tracks.

There was some big sedan, black as a bull, in the rearview mirror. It was riding our bumper, trying to muscle past us on the narrow, slippery road. I didn't shout, I didn't say a single word, and better still—I left her to deal with it on her own.

Again, a horn—she glanced at me for a second, then looked straight ahead. There was nowhere to pull over, to the left was the ravine, to the right a wall of snow. At the next bend the black coffin-like silhouette once again jumped into the mirror and passed us, flashing its headlights. It almost scraped our door, but she kept the car steady and didn't hit the brakes. "Pig!" she shouted in a shaking voice and wrapped her fingers tighter around the wheel, helpless. I got a look at the guy: driving alone, a dark silhouette behind dark windows. The glass and the black shiny body of the car were freshly washed, you could even see the license plate—special issue with sixes at the beginning and end like all the gangsters.

A heavy truck appeared from around the bend, sanding the highway. The black car was blocking the road, driving straight down the middle without budging. The truck began to honk hoarsely, from the bed a guy in a hat with earflaps angrily waved a shovel. At the last second the car swerved to the side, its right tires jumping onto the icy embankment. Then it plowed through a piled-up snow bank where the top of a wooden bus stop sign was jutting out. The driver of the black car laid on the horn, as if he had had the right to do all that, and then disappeared into the falling blanket of snow.

The truck had stopped, its driver was cursing. She slowed down; I told her to pull over and stop, too. We pulled over where there was a small shoulder and just sat there, without getting out. Directly in front of us I could see the battered sign that the guy had mowed down along with the snow bank. We each smoked a cigarette. We drove on.

We saw him a few miles further on. He had stopped, again smack in the middle of the highway. He was pissing, but he hadn't waded into the fresh snow between the trees. It only now occurred to me that he might be drunk. But I couldn't tell, he was standing still. He was simply a silhouette in a black leather jacket against the silhouette of a black car.

I saw it all clearly, I realized that we would pass him and in a little while he'd be riding our ass again. But what I did at that moment wasn't premeditated. What I'm trying to say is that I did it as knee-jerk hooliganism, not as a way to get rid of him in the following miles. Whatever it was, something just came over me and I quickly rolled down the window. The sound of the motor came in along with the white snowy air, but somehow it was still quiet. She was also silent; she just looked at me. I picked up the bottle of water that had been rolling around at my feet. It was heavy and full of ice, having frozen underneath the seats overnight.

I stuck my arm out the window and swung—so hard that my elbow smacked into the doorframe. The bottle went flying and, without my having taken precise aim, hit the windshield of the man's car. It shattered and turned white, crumbling into pieces. "Drive," I said in a small voice, rolling up the window as fast as I could. She hit the gas.

In the following moments I thought I would die. My arms and legs shook wildly, but my brain worked like a machine. The broken glass and the oncoming snow, the wind—there's no way he'd be able to drive with all that whipping in his face. He wouldn't be able to, or so I hoped. She passed a semi that was spewing fine icy ash out from under its tires, mixed with salt and sand. No, without a windshield he wouldn't be going anywhere, the snowstorm was our ally. Just like the sheet of ice covering the car that also hid our license plate number. I looked at my phone, no reception. So there's no way he could call and have somebody lie in wait for us. Besides, he was alone—hadn't I seen him through those tinted windows?

It wasn't easy to calm down, and I failed to do so in any case. My heart was pounding painfully, but at least I refused to be scared of what would happen. I felt a pleasant warmth wash over my whole body. It seemed like the car's feeble heater was roaring, I took off my jacket. She looked at me from time to time, smiling.

I think she drove more recklessly than she ever had. That morning on those icy curves even sixty miles per hour was too fast, but she somehow managed to get us to the city in less than an hour.

Like I said, that was the first time. But no matter what we tried after that, she painstakingly guarded me from the thought of K-shev, from the transformation of the game into reality. That meant sacrificing herself constantly, coming between me and him when he got in the way, if only as an image. That is, *him* as an image, not her. Her as a body, absolutely real. From the very beginning.

>>>

We pushed our way through the swarm of cars in front of the underground garage. Above us the ventilation pipes were spewing out steam, the melting snow was dripping, the hoods of the cars were smoking. Early risers were coming out of the garage, only we were going in, underground. The lowest level was the cheapest, we followed the ramps downward for a long time. Most of the spots in the checkered space gaped empty between the dirty-white lines. She parked, turned off the engine and the lights. The automated light on the cement ceiling went out, leaving only the faint bulbs above the exit and the illuminated arrow pointing to the stairs. She leaned back against the seat and turned her head toward me.

"Take off your clothes," she said and closed her eyes.

I hadn't moved, I was just sitting there when she leaned in and looked at me up close:

"So you think you're really brave, huh?"

"No," I answered in a voice that I myself could barely hear.

"Shut up!" she said and grabbed my chin between her fingers. "Do you know what could've happened? They could've beaten you like a dog. Cut you up into little pieces and dumped you somewhere. And me, too. Me, too!" She wrestled out of her jacket, pulled up her shirt, and squeezed her breasts in her hands, right in front of me, in front of my face.

Before, when we were on the highway, and afterward, I clearly realized what could happen. But in that split second, which remained the most real moment of the whole incident—in the darkness underground, in that darkened, hollow crypt with a flat ceiling—there the horror of it all suddenly came together in one place. It thickened up as if in a syringe and gushed into all the corners of my body, right down to the core of my bones. Instead of fear and panic, however, I felt something impossible. It couldn't be stopped, at that second I wasn't afraid that I was crushing her violently in my arms. And she pulled my hair so hard I could hear the roots creaking inside my skull as if they were being torn out of the skin. I think that no matter how hard she bit my neck and shoulders, even if she had done it harder, I still wouldn't have felt pain, only the dizzying rocking we were locked into. She slapped me across the face, for an instant her nails scratched me—and between every slap she kissed me. She whispered in fits and starts, barely pausing for breath: "My darling! . . . My darling!" And her teeth bit into lips, mine or hers.

>>>

"He also made off with a lot of money, right?" The question was posed voicelessly, but she had heard it before, from my very self, from inside. She shuddered, but the jerk with which her body suddenly pushed me away didn't let on to what she had felt.

New gangsters had now seized K-shev's cars, they had taken control of the entire black automotive fleet. Today they enjoy the luxuries we all railed against in unison on the cold nights of the protests. With a husky blow of its horn, a somber sedan passes by the frost-covered cars of the fugitive wretches, the secret lovers who have snuck out of the city, incognito.

I won't deny that the thought of K-shev sometimes also transformed into the idea of money. But that wasn't the main thing. Truth be told, there was no *main thing*. If you're expecting me— and rightfully so—to talk about a crime, it's still very difficult to clarify the basic motive.

Interrogation/Lexicon

1.) What's your favorite color?
Red.

2.) Whom do you love?
Blood.

3.) Not *what*, but *whom*.

Don't you get it?—I love, down to the blood.

>>>

I toss a few more scraps of paper into the fire, pages torn out of lined notebooks. The light blazes on her face, like a smile.

I tell her: "We've had a fun, easy time lately, haven't we?"

She nods. That smile on her lips. I really could swear that she is the most ordinary girl in the world, simply sitting there, motionless, enjoying the sun made of flames. We're out basking in the sunshine.

I tell her: "The only thing I have any regrets about is that there's no way for us to reach the very end, *there*, together."

"Where? The sea?"

"Not the sea, the sky," I reply after a short pause.

This isn't love, I know, and words have begun to take on far too much significance.

"You know what?" she says, "I want to go home."

Fine. I stand up. I pick up the backpack and sling it onto my back. I've got a long descent ahead of me. "Don't leave me now," she says, "don't go."

"Where would I go? Just listen to yourself." I stroke her neck. I trace the curve of her ear with my fingers. She leans her head to the side and squeezes my hand between her shoulder and cheek.

"What's wrong? Did I upset you?" I whisper, while trying to catch her face between my palms, but she keeps turning her head from side to side. As if she's playing, she's smiling, but I can see tears flowing from her eyes. From under her motionless eyelids, sealed shut with Band-Aids, these droplets are creeping out— when I lick them, they taste like a camp drugstore, like a bandage.

Now that's it, today I can finally say that I've perfected my notion of the face of a girl who is suffering and who is beautiful because of it. In its pristine whiteness, her hidden gaze cannot reflect me, this angel can't see me, I'm not here, for a moment at least I don't deserve my well-deserved punishment. And for that reason her perfect body attracts me twice as strongly. I slide my hands under her shirt, she hiccups and sobs in a choked voice. But the rope wound around her body digs into the skin beneath her breasts, I can't reach any farther down.

This isn't love, of course, and it's starting to get out of hand. Nevertheless, something always has to be done about desire. The rope is wrapped around the tree trunk, a few loops and a firmly tied knot at the end. Only her legs are free. "Goodbye," I tell her, as if wanting to escape my own presence. Then I jerk apart her ankles, her heels, which had been planted on the ground on rubber soles.

I sink into her, just as I am, backpack and all, we collapse into each other, but this time I don't sense the stalking that always trips me up before the end—the gaze, the eyes from the portrait on the wall. When we had tiptoed in, without knowing, however, that we'd have to break the silence even if we didn't want to.

Her eyes are sealed shut, her hands are tied, she can scream if she wants, I purposely left her mouth free. But she doesn't even make a sound now, she'll only scream at the very end. For the first time since I've made love out in the open and consciously, it happens: everything in me manages to focus itself straight ahead and to the end. We come inside each other, fused, numb. She screamed at the end after all, simultaneously in despair and ecstasy.

The idea of bringing her to the final control point, CP 0, was not, in fact, new; it had crossed my mind before. I'd thought about it— as I had with most of the others, by the way. But I had never done it with any of them until now—never, not since I had discovered the zero point within the system of coordinates. The place where everything begins and ends.

Time, during which we're sufficiently free to be able to *play* K-shev. With no qualms, at that. But now, at this age, games have become dangerous.

Interrogation/Game

1.) What's your name?
   You know it.

2.) What do your parents do?
   C'mon, cut it out.

3.) How old are you?
   How old am I?—I've reached the age when girls become a threat. You afraid?

"No," I reply after a pause.

Hopefully she won't be able to figure out whether I'm afraid that she started on her own, that she started first. Or whether I'm happy about it.

"C'mon, ask, I know you want to."

"Fine. Why did they send us there? That time, back then."

"Where?"

"You know where. For the tests."

"They were preventative measures."

"But why didn't everyone go, why only me?"

"We couldn't send everyone. We didn't want to stir up mass panic."

"So why me in that case, since it wasn't dangerous? And what about the others, tell me about the other people's kids."

"I did it for my personal reassurance, I had to be sure."

"I remember how they would bring us food, only milk and bread for a whole month—from a village, from somewhere really far away, right? 'Clean food,' that's what you called it. But what about the others? What about their children? Was their food clean?"

"I had to make an important decision, I had to be sure. I needed to know that everything was okay with you."

"They ran through the grass, they walked in the rain, they were all out at the May Day demonstrations—couldn't you have at least spared them that, was it really necessary?"

"I don't understand what you're talking about."

"Would it have been such a big deal for you to tell people not to drink milk and not to pick anything from the trees? To at least forbid them from swimming in rivers and the sea until the danger had passed?"

Silence. She begins again: "Do you think you're going to get away with it? Do you think that nobody has found out about it and nothing is known about it? Don't try to tell me that they didn't inform you, don't try to tell me you were misled—who sent me there for a check up? Why don't you just admit that you did it on purpose—which means you had your doubts, you were afraid! Even back then you wanted it to stay a secret, you only wanted to take care of yourself."

"I didn't take care of myself."

"To take care of yourself only and others like you, as for the rest—who cares what happens! It was a Sunday, you purposely chose Sunday, when there were no other people at that institute. They stripped me naked and put me through some machine . . ."

"They didn't put you through any machine."

"At the Institute of Radiology—did you think I didn't understand anything, did you think I couldn't read? Do you think I'm just a child, you're counting on that, right? Me being a child and not understanding."

"You're not a child, of course. Children don't speak that way to their parents."

"Shut up! Shut up, just stop talking, you're making me sick. All you do is talk and talk and stroke your chin like that, making that face. I'm not like the rest, I'm not like the others—I know you. I know, get it? And the others know, how do you think you're going to wriggle out of it, to get away with it? You're hoping to get away scot-free after committing a crime!"

If only she could move her arms, I tell myself, if only she could hit me.

"You're imagining things, you're making things up. Tell me, do you really believe that I'm a criminal, that I could do something to hurt someone? And if so, what?"

"Don't use me as an excuse."

"Just tell me what!"

"Don't try to use me. You always do that—you use me."

"You know I've always only done what's best for you. If you stop to think about it, if you finally learn to think, you'll realize that everything I've done was for you and because of you."

"But I don't want that!"

"Think about it."

"I don't want to think!"

"See, what did I tell you?"

"Don't start with that again. Don't keep telling me to think, don't keep tormenting me."

"Who, me?"

"I can't, I can't do it like this . . ."

She can't think like this, I know. Her thoughts break up, get cut off, they short-circuit.

"You can't do this anymore, I forbid you."

"Who, me? Am I the one doing this? So now you're accusing *me*?"

"You have no right!"

"I know I have no right. So why is it happening all over again, why has it ended up like that? What are you doing here in front of me? Get the hell out of here!"

"No."

If only she could really get the hell out of here. If only she could not be here. If only she could take a swing and hit me, but so hard that I would fly back, far away from her face. I'd be torn away from her presence, lose consciousness, the end—for her to stop existing. If only she, not me, would disappear and melt away, cease.

"This is a crime, this is something that shouldn't be done! I'm your daughter!"

She doesn't hit me, however, she just prolongs the moment. So I'm forced to hit her myself.

She screams, but not aloud, not out loud—her body curls inwardly and then erupts again: "Why did you do that?"

The question that destroys me. It pierces me and makes me wince. And she repeats it: "Why did you do that do me? Why did you do it?"

Her arms grow shorter, her knees, pressed against my knees, turn into narrow disks that desperately try to kick me, her body shrinks in my hands. She pummels me with her little fists, her hands with their childish nails are frenzied with rage. Night is falling, it's raining, the nightmare thickens. I fall with her in my arms, I fall on top of my very self.

Her body slowly passes beneath the edge of the leaden cliffs. It is swallowed up, both of us are swallowed up by the pyramid, the gray squares stacked up without a crack.

"Just a few more minutes," says the doctor, a professor of something or other, von Ehrenbauer. "Just a few more minutes, Herr K-shev, and the test results will be ready."

Leukemia was the mildest punishment I expected to befall me—for everything I had done.

>>>
It smells horrible.

The river is murky, black lines parallel to the current. Muddy shafts and fuses flit past, matted balls of paper pop up in the eddies. Slimy, frayed rags of unknown consumer origin lap at the furry, sticky rocks. Rough bristles line the canal's cement walls. It's not even a river, but actually a canal, the longest reinforced canal in Sofia, narrow and straight as a gutter, cutting straight through the settlement: The Perlovska River.

The intestine-river flows swiftly, as if it can't wait to carry off the shameful filth somewhere—where?—somewhere else. However, I return once more to that place, cast out of the illusion that I was ever anywhere at all.

The dream of escape crumples in my hands, nothing but a cheap wrapper. The scent of vomit at my feet invades it like a signal of reality, even though I myself was the one who vomited here, see, that's the juice from my innards—which, by the way, simply confirms yet again that reality is something entirely internal. I always run this far and stop here, at the bridge over the river. The canal, slippery stones on both sides of the channel.

>>>

Did I fail? Of course—but that's a feeling that helps me hang on: at least on the edge, at least for a bit.

You are the reason words exist, as I admitted before, and now I'll admit that even if no one among you can help me, I still respect you, I bow passionately before every *yes* that extends the path through fear in the face of every *no* that could stop me.

So here I am in shoes, tube socks, and ridiculous, non-sporty shorts. The journey continues, the running continues, begun at the roots of the night only to hit the light from the iris of the sun itself.

The guys at the reception desk only briefly lifted their heads when I flew through the door's revolving wings and entered via the hotel's electric lobby into the natural darkness of the night. The cold metal vase of the Elba, knocked over onto the ground, flowed to one side. The water, the pontoon bridge, the pathway— I remember, that much I remember clearly—that I'm running, right? Please say *yes*, please fix me to this game board for at least a little while longer with the pin that I have been preserved on.

>>>

It turned out that the sign for Makarenko Strasse really marked a street with that name, and not just a nightmare in my head. What's more, further on I also discovered a school also named after the Soviet pedagogue. So it would be bad manners not to reach the end. A thousand meters or so to the clinic. After all, we're talking about money, a whole briefcase-full, a million and a half.

>>>

I enter quietly, I enter slowly—that's how a needle should find a vein. It's early, the hallways are empty. There's a white splotch in front of his door, light coming from a window built way up into the ceiling for some unknown reason. This strange Hamburgian and Saxon architecture. But whatever, it doesn't matter. I don't pay too much attention to the hospital design—if nothing else, I'm still a medical student. Who never graduated.

Medicine
My choice, not accidental, as always. The demon with the ruby-red eyes—I'll admit my naïveté—I wanted to conquer it with my own two hands.

So medicine it was, that's where we met. She was looking for the same thing I was—the same self-absorbed image of that which *kills everything*. The death-demon is always exactly your same age.

During our lectures in anatomic pathology we were always in the front row, right by the dissection table. The yellow gloves I'd wear—too plastic, non-surgical, with no intention of saving anybody from anything. The body, already progressing beyond the fated stages, crossing over into chemistry—it no longer had anything to do with biology.

That's where we met—I couldn't help noticing her gaze, which never strayed from the instructor's hands, never blinked. I liked isolating myself from the group, I would take notes, ignoring the groans of fainting female classmates and the huffing of everyone else who was waiting for this foul-smelling trial—and their entire course of study—to finally be over, so they could rush into the pristine and private practices of their dreams—without blood, if possible, full of well-guarded and wealthy clients.

Like she told me, she wanted to become a pediatrician. The first lie, although I wouldn't say she was lying to me. She, of course, was always completely sincere—but she was fooling herself.

>>>

I'll admit it, I had a dream that we were going down the white staircase toward the anatomy lab at night. I already know that childhood memories are ineffaceable. But both in childhood and in the youth of a profession, life-changing discoveries are also etched on the memory: tastes, smells, accidental touches, indescribable movements, sometimes overpowering and concrete. However, don't believe for a second, don't expect me to say that we cut things up (even if only in my dream), that we sliced off little pieces, organs and limbs, from the unfeeling corpses and that we nibbled on them, testing the flavor—no.

Don't expect me to say anything more than that—it's just a dream, right?

>>>

They admitted me the third time I applied, but kicked me out by my second year. Chemistry was always terrible—not just for me, but terrible in and of itself, even when I managed to cleverly copy the problems on the entrance exam. I knew that chemistry would find a way to take revenge on me for that scam.

The professor wasn't impressed by my deep yet rather narrow knowledge of one specific section of the periodic table: the radioactive isotopes. It's a little too early for you to be curing leukemia, young man. Set aside the actinoids for now, let's first focus on some of the simpler elements from the first group: potassium, sodium, lithium, and best of all—hydrogen.

Go to hell, I should've told him, but I knew that he, too, was just another naïve sucker, an innocent adversary. He was trying to make himself seem important—Mendeleev and the periodic table give you the sense of superiority, as if somebody *up there* has revealed life's big secrets to you. The strength of the periodic law.

Yes, young man, The Law is very important, it takes precedence over the little boxes in the table. We can still add on as many little boxes as we want, but the principle is the crucial thing. What is chemistry? We can only understand this by contemplating what an element is. And what is a chemical element, young man?

"A chemical element"—I decide to give him an insolent and absolutely by-the-textbook answer—"is a substance that cannot be broken down or changed into another substance by *chemical* means. Yes, but by other, *physical* means, on the atomic level—that's where the really exciting changes happen—and what changes they are! Just like every sickness, by the way, radiation sickness is also more of a blessing than a curse. But if I were to spell it out for you, especially for you, it might very well blow your mind. Because radiation arrives in a ray of unearthly beauty, my dear professor, with a hint of the cosmos and a headstrong character. It can't be compared with any other force—it's corporal, yet incorporeal. And invisible. It's a foreign substance, yet it permeates into this world boundlessly, because it arrives in waves, and the world as a whole is wavelike, woven out of sinusoids. Its colors excite the eyes. Sounds, aural stimulation, vibrate on the eardrums. Scents, undulating aromas, mobile abstract surges of information, television, radio—a vital stream of fluids!"

Thrown out of the auditorium, I stop in the empty hallway next to the milky-white, paint-smeared window. On the window ledge, on top of the layers of dust, lie the bodies of dead mosquitoes, right in front of the screen. Dead of their own accord. I see two that continue holding their pose—it's deceptive, as if they could take flight again any second. I reach out, but they remain motionless. I blow on them, the bodies unexpectedly start crawling, far too easily. They look like decommissioned airplanes retired to some deserted airfield, left to time and to themselves. Take this one here, for example—it took off and landed, and afterward didn't make any other movement. No effort whatsoever to continue. Or perhaps effort was impossible, too strenuous. So that's it, game over—now it just sits in the same place, as if this act didn't cause it any particular suffering. Its body is still standing on its legs, it hasn't flipped over onto its back.

>>>

Again, a hallway. Now the door is not slamming behind my back, but is rather there in front of me: K-shev's room, which I have to enter, for something more than a visit.

I have to enter quietly, to enter slowly. With all my hatred and all my respect.

3

HER FATHER

THERE exist so-called *personal forms* of leukemia. Some of them
deserve to be studied with particular attention, above and beyond
the usual care for the sufferer. Certain leukemic syndromes are so
rare that they are named after the patient himself: the Leroi Syndrome or Leukemia Familiae Jacobsen. So why shouldn't there be
a *K-shev Leukemic Syndrome*—strange, but not impossible, right?
German medicine could make a new and decisive breakthrough at
his expense, while Hamburg could surpass Tubingen and the Max
Planck Institute in terms of glory. And K-shev himself would be
immortalized in the process. I would guess they're already at it,
they can't help but notice something strange, something unusual
in the arresting pathogenic mechanism. Something that renders
useless the gas-transporting blood cells, pumped out of the heart
of The Boss.

But such a finding isn't enough, the Nobel Prize is not award-
ed for a diagnosis alone—despite sympathetic leanings, despite

the fact that the nomination committee knows that Hamburg was where Alfred Nobel founded his Dynamit AG, Alfred Nobel & Co—the oldest factory for explosives in the world.

No, a breakthrough is needed, an explosion—the prize rewards overcoming. The explosion clears away obstructions, so afterward you can pass by freely. However, I'm not sure whether certain postwar-German complexes would allow the doctors here to catch sight of such a solution. But I know, it's all clear to me.

So—in his arm, in the crook of his elbow, there's a shunt. A transparent tube leads to the IV drip from its other end. I pull it out—the needle is way too thick, I guess I should've expected that. It might hurt, but I don't have a choice now, there's no time. I press the tip into my skin, right above the vein. Quiet! Quietly and slowly. Pain, just as I expected. But whatever, it's nothing to cry about. I've waited so long, I've retraced this path so many times, now we're only separated by a few feet of medical grade rubber, the sterile tubing, like a weapon. It guarantees the attack—a pure-blooded memory, without the interference of impurities, without the presence of outsiders—just Comrade K-shev and I, just you and I.

His eyes open somehow in slow motion—has he recognized me? I thought he was sleeping, I thought he would leave his interior only with difficulty. Does he remember me?

Pumping my fist provides the initial, necessary surges. The red ribbon crawls into the transparent corridor. The blood reaches his vein. Expecting the end, he could hardly have hoped for such a final self-sacrifice. Well, Comrade K-shev, obviously there are moments when even your fabricated ideology bears fully ripened fruit, full-blooded, that is. Now it's my turn, now the hemoglobin in me will do the rest—disease added to disease doesn't always mean twice the disease—you only live once. Perhaps it means a cure, perhaps survival. Perhaps going back over the boundary, beyond which responsibility loses its meaning. Life, in one of its strange forms, is suffering—I give it back to you now, Comrade K-shev. I, one little Pioneer, the only one who did not turn traitor and consign you to oblivion. You can live, breathing oxygen through the radioactive cells that we now share. By your gaze I can tell that you weren't expecting it. Yes, coming out of a coma is painful, no doubt about it. Why does it always work out such that happiness can't be had without just a little more suffering? And not without you: *not without you* also means not without your definitive destruction—you understand what I'm getting at. Revenge has to play out its endgame. I'm listening, I'm waiting for the whole truth, my ears are sizzling with impatience. Comrade K-shev?

>>>

The Boss's circulatory system envelops us, every one of us. The queen bee attracts her drones. The sun rises and sets, the goal is visible during the daylight hours, but once night falls, we stagger around in the numbing darkness, flapping our arms like wings, but without the elevating power. A slow falling, my body grows pale, emptiness frosts over my veins.

My blood is no longer inside me, it has crept out, yet it's pleasant somehow—like an obligation being lifted. I can't feel myself.

But what do I sense in this case, whom do I feel?

>>>

He's dreaming now, the exhaustion before death is lapping at his body and every muscle. The magnified blossoms of the pumpkins, a bright, egg-yolk yellow—they jut out to the side above the splashes of green along the trellis. They're licking their viney chops, they'll drink him up with their mouths. And every drop of blood as well. I get off the motorcycle, kill the motor—I don't want him to hear me. He's dazed, I know—perhaps he's injured, but at the very least he's probably deathly tired after an all-night chase, in the rain. I left the gendarmerie, the dogs, the posse behind me, I'm going on alone, I'm going first.

There he is—it isn't easy for him to hide. I catch sight of droplets on the rocks, red drops of fear, red drops of death. Not his—killers always leave traces behind them in the blood of their victims. In just a short while I myself will rise like the sun, after taking the shot. I take out the pistol. I know there's at least one bullet left, I'm sure of it. The blue cartridge glints in the hole of the chamber, like the gap from a pulled tooth, and the hammer glows whitish-silver from up above.

His head—resting against the wall, leaning back and to the side, his cheek propped against a sack. The hemp rope encircles its edges like a pillow under a corpse's skull. Should I fire point-blank, from a few feet away? In the chest or neck? The last cartridge, the last bullet, the last drop of my blood. A lone fugitive, the only one left. Not quite killed off yet, the last guerrilla.

The tube shifts—the transparent piping that connects the still-breathing chunks of flesh in some strange way—the blood in his blood, the blood in my blood. This is the end, which means that the long chase is coming to a close.

Like twins of an evened-out age, the bodies hooked up to the IV find their center, the golden mean.

As I'm killing you
I might resemble, too
a star that is
finishing its flight.

As I'm killing you
I might be dying, too—
but death is also
a form of life.

I can't deny it, *Blondy*, I can't help but admit after everything that's happened, that I, too, used to sing along with the Argirovi Brothers.

In the golden mean, the silver of my blood, like electrolysis, welds together the twins in me and in him.

>>>

In Hamburg the lioness at the Hagenbeck Zoo startles, pricks up her ears. Victim, prey or carcass? K-shev is sick, far too unwell for his bodily remains to be fed to the king of predators. As for the crocodiles—why not? Those prehistoric reptiles can digest everything, evolution itself passes through their stomach and intestines.

He knows, of course, that in the end his corpse will have to be buried. Now I understand why he picked Hamburg of all places—not because of the quality of the medical care. And not because of the Reeperbahn. The reason lies in the uniqueness of the Ohlsdorf Cemetery: the largest graveyard in Europe, covering 400 hectares, and the largest in the world. Here you can really get lost, be nobody. However, he'll be of no use to me anonymous.

>>>

Only a short while remains until morning, only a short while until sunrise, washed in a radioactive haze. Just the physical luminary that spews life and under which life crackles as if electrified. We're standing in long rows in front of the granite pedestal. Music blares through the loudspeakers, and our shoulders touch—mine and the shoulder beneath the white blouse of the girl next to me. I don't know her name, but if we were alone right now, even right here out of the open, under all that music and those lights, with the convenient untying of our Pioneer neckerchiefs that is even prescribed in the manual for the ceremony . . . And if our shirts went as well . . . And if after that . . .

But then the drape covering the monument is pulled away, terribly slowly and irreversibly. You aren't ready—no matter how much you've prepared, and despite the fact that you're expecting it, can you really be ready?—the cover slips off, falling like a sheet revealing the body of a dead man for his loved ones to identify. It's him all right, no doubt about it, the sculptor has captured a striking resemblance. With the help of characteristic details. By means of perspective. K-shev, cast in metal—it's terrible.

To tell you the truth, I know that in the end his death will rob me of everything. It will leave me only the monuments, from which you can't demand accountability, not for anything.

>>>

Since his corpse really does need to be buried, for hygienic reasons at the very least—I'm forced to make a decision. However, on the other hand, due to certain personal, historical reasons of my own, it's important that we wait until *she* is convinced that it's true. To that end, even if only temporarily, the most convenient solution is the mausoleum.

The Mausoleum

Everyone else goes to visit loved ones in some normal way—to the neighboring street, to the country or to a near or a faraway city. Even abroad, if they've managed to maximally distance themselves from familial circles.

We, however, visit "Daddy"—my father-in-law, in fact—in the heart of the nation, at the foot of the very citadel of power.

"Let's go see Daddy again," she'll say.

"Fine, let's go," I'll reply.

And shove my fist into my pocket.

I don't have a father, she had told me. Now, when the dream is on the way to becoming a reality, she cries absolutely unexpectedly, at every entering. I don't like it, but whatever—I'm the last one, who. What can I say?

>>>

The mausoleum is cold. Cold and always empty when I go with her to *see Daddy*. Special visiting hours, a sliver of space arranged by the authorities for the intimate seclusion of family members, direct descendents. Despite this luxury, they don't allow me to bring flowers—even relatives are forbidden from doing so. Such a gesture on my part is self-serving, of course, as it would allow me to stick my nose in the filter of roses and distance myself a bit from the oppressive smell spilling out around us. Posthumous aftershave, a sweet perfume, wafting out from under his armpits.

"Your daddy is a corpse," I feel like telling her, "your daddy died a long time ago and stinks," I feel like screaming at her. "If we'd left him to rot like all the others, there'd be nothing left of him by now. Just a few bones and a skull for you to keep your pencils in. Just take a whiff, don't you smell that stench? His skin has been rotting for years, they shine it up and steam it, they polish it, but it rots and thins out. So that it doesn't tear, they cover it with talcum powder, which mixes together with the putrefaction, the talcum powder decays along with the skin."

They've taken out his intestines, his lungs and his whole brain through his nose—but the skin remains. Beneath his eyelids there are glass balls, translucent, greenish and translucent, they didn't even bother drawing fake eyes on them—the skin remains, however, it's real and it stinks. And even though they keep sticking hairs into his scalp over and over again—they keep falling out.

In the darkness the guards whisper in a strained voice, startling the paralyzed visitors: "Move along!"—move along, they say, so that no one will see the hair slowly falling from his head. And afterward they'll spend the whole night putting it back on. He has no right to sleep, your father.

I'm going to be sick, I say, I'm going to be sick, I want to leave.

>>>

Truth be told, he looks a little like a cosmonaut under that oval orb placed over his head. His skull is covered with stretched skin, strained, yellowed like parchment. He steals even in death—but you're not going to take away my final dream, too, I tell him, you're not going to snatch it away!

Yes, I was little at the time, and I didn't understand. But I sensed it clearly, only the lack of suitable words prevented me from creating a strong argument for Comrade Todorov during our class on morals or ethics or law, whatever it was. Because now I know that he would've understood me.

"And what is the point of going into the cosmos?" He had asked me, peering through the thick lenses of his glasses.

"The cosmos is infinite." That's how I should've answered him, maybe I even really said it.

But I didn't know how to continue. I couldn't see how simple the ending was:

"Yes, infinite. And after every happy event gapes the end of happiness. Lonely people are lonely only in restricted space, but in infinity—no loneliness exists there, either. There, horror reigns."

>>>

I understand why she's crying like that, why she doesn't leave. They turn out the lights, night slithers across the marble. But she continues standing there, not moving. She must be remembering something, the two of them have their memories—here's one historical fact, the only one that cannot be changed. I admit, after everything that's happened, that fate in all its stubbornness always manages to place me—sometimes even on my knees holding a bouquet of flowers—in front of some incredibly trifling yet incorrigible detail, such as this one: she is nevertheless *his daughter*.

Nostalgia

She remembered how during the storm, the somersaulting waves would surge over the bridge, pouring onto the shore. On such days she wasn't allowed to go near the sea. The sand, wet not from rain, but from drops of flying foam. She had gotten used to it, there were always lots of guards around. The men often changed and she persistently asked them:

"What's your name?"

The man shifts his startled gaze from the girl in the red or white dress with white or red polka-dots. The unknown man looks at the other man, whom she knows. Her father, the man whom she knows, nods. The stranger smiles awkwardly, but takes the gesture as an order. For what's probably the first time since he's started the job, he has to say his first name:

"Svilen."

"Dimitar." (Or perhaps *Mitko*, if it occurs to him to answer her in the way people usually talk to little girls.)

"Asen."

"Atanas."

"Valyo."

"Svilen." (Svilen again—strangely enough, there are two Svilens.)

Most of them don't have children yet, most sergeants from the security forces are quite young, "unattached," as is written in their official documents. More like soldiers than employees. With a small red card containing all the important information, in a holder with square flaps, like a pleather butterfly, kept in an inside pocket. From the wing's crease dangles a thin, sturdy string with a small safety pin at the end, which is used to attach the officer's ID to the lining of his jacket.

Once, a little piece of shell gets stuck under her fingernail. The girl is crying. Dimitar or Valentin or Svilen pulls out his ID card, with "Safety and Security" emblazoned across the top. He unfastens the pin and with its tip extracts the painful chip of mica. His fingers tremble slightly, afraid of hurting her. This fear for her envelops her. The painful particle releases her, returns to the other harmless grains of sand.

She remembers, her childhood is a string of points, of childish joys and pains. Childhood is an invisible projection in the rearview mirror. No big jolts, no out-of-the-ordinary pain, there was always someone to look after her. A breakfast of watermelon, soft feta cheese. The gate blocking the road at the end of the residence, beyond which entrance was forbidden. In the big, convex, circular mirror mounted on a post in the corner, both ends of the road were visible, crescent wings. No one came or went. No one arrived, besides the little girl in the polka-dot dress.

In her memory, there are dark and light shadows, spots of sun. She digs in with her fingers and lifts them up like a piece of cloth, flat carpets, under which there is nothing. Yet something did happen, something important. Something more than just a jab, more than a prick to the skin, a sliver in the tip of her finger. She places her hand in her palm, lies down for a while, tries to remember. But can't. In such moments she says *come here* and I enter, but she can't remember what, she can't discover it.

Now the residence is closed, empty, sealed up. The traces of its previous owner have evaporated, but the walls are still standing, the stones with the imprints of shells and the fossilized bodies of shrimp. She arrives here again, this time in cut-off shorts and with a backpack on her back, sandals on her dusty feet. She goes beyond, into the interior. The gate is rusty and probably doesn't work anymore. Of the guardhouse, all that remains is a shapely silhouette, windows boarded up, wire on the posts alongside it that at one time fenced off the road. Barbed wire on the grass, piled up in a rusty heap, a dog barking hoarsely. There is no guard, or at least there's none in sight. Yet going in is dangerous, as well as pointless—now the walls guard themselves, the stones easily give way underfoot. What a landslide the sandy cactus garden has become. Above the wings of the terraces with a view of the sea, rusty bedsprings jut out, the unfinished frame of a support wall, abandoned in mid-construction. Foul-smelling water, colorless, streams beneath the cement slabs. The round mirror at the curve hangs broken, with only a single surviving triangle, like part of the imaginary face of a watch that at some point felt the light between dawn and dusk creep across it. An image remained there, somewhere between four and six o'clock, strewn with specks. From behind, from the reflection itself, little brownish flowers have dripped down like the legs of birds living in the bottom of the picture, in a mirror-image world. Somewhere there the foam has been swallowed up, the waves have been drained away, somersaulting over the quay—she seemed to catch a glimpse of dolphins' bellies in the water—the past itself preserved in the craziest hours, between four and six in the afternoon. And one polka-dotted little girl with a dress of light and shadow—but her feet aren't visible, standing on the other side of the reflection—nothing is visible except the tears clouding up her eyes.

Oh, how sad that wonderful past has turned out to be. Because there is nothing in it that you can grasp onto, nothing for you to keep.

She feels like creating life, having a child, a daughter or a boy, better a little girl—but why, what for? To repeat everything, to rehash it? Why would she do it, for whom? For herself, or . . . For herself, right?

This simple discovery stops the very drops in her eyes. It's so empty inside that above such an abyss it's even useless to cry—there's simply nowhere for the tears to fall. There's no bottom.

>>>

It's clear to me—*nothing* should remain of him. In the sense that this very *nothing* should be buried and destroyed, this emptiness in which his image drowns time as if in a black hole.

Arranged in a square, fifty thousand one-hundred-euro bills—a million and a half—take up an area of one hundred and eighty square meters. Its symbolic, three-dimensional significance, however, can be far more electrifying.

He probably thinks he's pulled a fast one, shoving that much money into my hands. He hopes my heart will soften up, made extra-mushy by the anesthesia of wealth so I'll relent and release a respectable funerary sum. If for no other reason than to prevent him from appearing in my dreams. To leave him alone with the ground, consigned to eternity in a foreign city, as it were.

No, Comrade K-shev, that's not going to happen. I know your plans, I know them *deep down*. And I know, like I said before, I understand very well why you've chosen the cemetery in Hamburg.

Because:

The Elba, deep down, invisibly erodes the slippery abutments along its banks. Down at the foundations, near the concrete, underwater capitals that support the docks' pontoon skeleton—the longest pontoon structure in Europe—there the water finds cracks, twisting into eddies. It sucks down the dust of bodies from the ever-replenished supply of dead buried nearby in the four hundred hectares of the Ohlsdorf Cemetery, the largest burial park on the planet.

He dreams of lying there now, beneath a slab reading K-shev, comforted by the reassurances of gravediggers with traditions that he has found peace for all eternity, and in good company: Elise Brahms, and the great composer's sister; the Africanist Hans Schomburgk; and Karl Hein, the 1936 Olympic gold medalist in the hammer throw.

Like every one else, K-shev, too, will set off along the surges of the river, he'll head north. At Cuxhaven, the continent's exit, he'll take a turn. He'll flow out into the North Sea, along the Island of Neuwerk, frozen at its mouth, plunging deep under the sea's waters in the fairway of the local currents.

Particles of sand, dead epidermal cells, stones from a bladder clogged from years of sedentary living, from kidneys. Deficient red blood globules, the overly enlarged cancer cells of a leukemic circulatory system—the dead, sick man is travelling, swept out in an unknown direction. He slips away from me, away from my revenge—if such a goal still even exists.

Of course it exists!

If I'm not suspicious of K-shev even *in death*, that means I haven't learned anything. And then the whole path up to this point would have been pointless, wasted effort.

The dead man's bones embrace the mournful dust of opera singers and conductors, seafaring merchants and circus owners. Invisible and again omnipotent, he puts the final touch on his plans. He reaches out his hands, spreads his fingers. He takes a hostage, he takes in his death the life and work of the most important Nobel laureate buried in Ohlsdorf Cemetery: Gustav Hertz. Now I'm starting to understand, it's all clear.

Tombstone
Gustav Ludwig Hertz
(* 22. Juli 1887; † 30. Oktober 1975)
Born in Hamburg, buried in Hamburg.

The father and pioneer of quantum mechanics, winner of the Nobel Prize. The most important German trophy scientist, exiled by the Red Army to Sukhumi, on the Black Sea coast.

Leader of the Institute for Separation of *Uranium Isotopes*.

Winner of the Stalin Prize, member of the Soviet Union's Academy of Sciences.

"Damn," I say to myself—damn!

Only here, only now, do I begin to understand.

The Atomic Alliance

The sun peeks out, having slipped away from the labyrinth of the horizon, wet and radioactive, above the water of the rivers and the northern bays. The Atomic Alliance—a plot, a conspiracy. The enormous single atom, the sun above my head, which recycles its own light in disconsolate timelessness. A sun, displayed so as to signify absolute infinity. And the internal, invisible atoms that have entered into a secret pact with it. The particles that make up the whole, with scrupulous pedantry and sparing no details—the particles that I am made of. The structures in the construction of my body, the parts of the whole. I myself, along with thought, which remains without physical support, am located between them, stretched along the axis between the sun and my body.

>>>

He, the old man, makes love with the body of the motherland. This love gives birth to thousands of children and he organizes them into Pioneer battalions—attention! about-face!—he gives orders to the skittering legs of the surges, the Comsomol, and they all obey his every command. They live on his words and his voice, they hunger to resemble him, to imitate him in everything. But most of all his vices and weaknesses, the negative characteristics from his Party evaluations—it is these very things, the vices and weaknesses, which make the individual unique. Yet the leader's shortcomings, infinitely multiplied, turn the separate faces into a faceless mass. For this reason, he has the effect of an invisible illness, quasi-disintegration—I recognize him precisely because of this scattering.

Okay, it's clear, like we said: truly *nothing* should remain of him.

The Hamburg Crematorium
Part of the publicly traded company Hamburg Cemeteries
Fullsbütlerstrasse 756
22337 Hamburg

Price list and general information (valid as of January 1).

Built in 1965 and equipped with five cremation chambers with filtering systems for smoke collection according to the requirements in Regulation 27 on Gas Emissions in the Atmosphere. Open five days a week, with a twenty-four-hour cycle. Duration of a single cremation: sixty minutes at a temperature of 800-1,000°C. Capacity: 18,000 deceased annually. With subsequent storage in urns. Casketless cremations are not permitted. Package price, incl. urn and urn storage (for a maximum of 28 days)—281 euro.

Preparatory chamber—97 euro.

Medical examination in accordance with administrative requirements—51 euro.

Delivery of urn for burial in the neighboring cemetery (Hamburg region)—46 euro.

Total: 475, even though I feel like that's too much for him.

That leaves me with 1,499,525, plus or minus hotel expenses. Not bad, I figure.

>>>

I'm travelling, flying without layovers, resisting the temptation to sit in first class. By the way, I'm not raising all these financial questions out of self-interest—I'm not a cheapskate, I simply have to budget very carefully if I want things to end well.

But let's put that aside for now, at least for a bit—now there's the motherland, we're flying above the pale border that expresses her autonomy upon the earth.

This country, *The Motherland*, as seen from above, resembles a lion, a compact little creature with sturdy if rather short legs and neck, taken away due to the unsuccessful diplomacy and military policies of past regimes. Almost headless, the little lion races forward, as if wanting to flop into the waves of the sea that splashes its chest.

This humble territory's outlines don't hint at the silhouette of a serious nation. Nevertheless, besides a certain naïve charm, there is also dignity in them. Or perhaps I'm biased—I've known that map for far too long, from childhood, from the school blackboard, to be able to evaluate it objectively. I think I even hear K-shev's voice, calling from the luggage compartment:

> *My love for you is enough,*
> *my love for you is everything.*
> *I touch you through her, I embrace you,*
> *even if you don't love me.*

> *Land like a volcano-woman—*
> *But I don't need you any colder!*
> *I'm happy that your blood is southern,*
> *and your chastity belt forged from iron.*

I have no idea what he's talking about, I've already learned to tune out his jabber.

"After all is said and done, my boy," he continues, from the urn, "you still don't know anything. And to be perfectly honest, I, for my part, don't know anything anymore either, that's what it looks like to me. Okay, for example: you fly back and forth, travel around. But in the end you still have to go back home, hrrrr," K-shev sneezes and coughs hoarsely.

I know it's cold in the luggage compartment.

"Yes, and there we'll meet again. You'll pay for your bad behavior. Yes, because we'll meet up. I've laid out all the paths, my boy. Look: especially now, when I'm becoming *nothing*, shadow and smoke, like the shadows of the trees along the highway. Look, you can see it clearly from here, the asphalt encircles the homeland, its blue bandoliers crisscross the gardens' fruitful breasts. I'm beyond the sunflowers, I abide in the branches' shadow, I glow eternally at the curve in the road. The future that I'm shining from never becomes the past because:

> *We are at every kilometer,*
> *and on and on—until the end of the world!*

"Yes, you're right, you're absolutely right," I tell him to get him to shut up. I wrap myself up in the blanket. The vodka warms me pleasantly because it's pure and good, made by our brothers—these are former Soviet airlines, after all. Arrival in Kazakhstan: on time.

The Third Bulgarian Cosmonaut

To buy a trip to the cosmos, to pay a million and then some for it—I'm proud of this idea. But I need to be completely prepared, physically as well as financially. Medical exams, yes, and all those procedures.

The leader of the pre-launch cycle—Shatrov, Valentin Ivanovich—arrives on his bicycle, which is about twenty years old, Ukraine brand. The chain is always well greased. He carries the folders and training charts in a lovingly preserved plastic bag with the West Cigarettes logo on it and handles that have worn thin. There's no longer any need for me to be amazed, it would be terribly impolite in any case—not by the state of his bag or his shirt or his ratty jacket with its frayed sleeves. The glasses sitting on his nose—plastic frames, a unisex model with bifocal lenses—are held together on one side by a Band-Aid wrapped around the broken rivet.

In this unchanging form, Shatrov sits behind mountains of equipment that can conquer gravity or that, under different circumstances, could set off a fatal intercontinental war. He spins in the chair, covered in plaid upholstery that sticks up here and there at the edges of the back rest. He observes the censors, fills in the charts with a cheap pen, and in that unmistakable, soft Russian way gives me directions over the microphone, which is as gray as an antique cartridge. The microphone hangs at the end of an even grayer cord—that gray left in the past along with Bakelite and tube televisions. Insulation material made fragile by time, sclerotic arteries that have lost their elasticity—they are no longer manufactured in any chemical factory anywhere in the world. They've been replaced by modern rubber, ultra-flexible, which doesn't slide between your fingers even when it's sweaty.

But I, in a jumpsuit under the spacesuit, am sweating buckets. The inside of the uniform isn't padded, there are no ventilation holes along the seams or in the underarms or thighs. The humbleness of it all, the old-fashionedness, the wear-and-tear—it doesn't worry me, on the contrary—it inspires me. I know, I'm convinced it'll launch me into those dark heights over our heads with sufficient safety. And there will be so many stars up there that everything brought along from earth will lose its significance.

The old emblems haven't even been torn off the jumpsuits. Gold letters over the blue silky image: a round planet embroidered between wreaths of wheat, with the inscription "USSR." This reminds me of how, during the 1950s, K-shev had tried *to unite us* with the Soviet republics on the sly. Now, Mr. First Secretary, we can try again together.

>>>

I received a full set of clothing taken out of storage, still in rustling cellophane wrappers. I have underwear with strong seams that gives off some old smell, maybe camphor. Pure cotton, cream-colored, like ivory. Also T-shirts, with three-quarter-length sleeves. Shoes, socks without heels, and a pair for running that go all the way to the knee. The pants have little slits for attaching the small galvanized hooks at the end of the belts, which connect at the lower back to something like a seat—almost like a diaper of soft cloth, but green instead of white and as furry as an astrakhan. Thus wrapped, I sit in the hollowed-out shell of the training chair. Then in the catapult. The gray jacket is short in the waist, while its collar is rubbery, somehow alive from the tension of the elastic sewn inside. Muscles of natural caoutchouc, I catch a whiff of its stinging scent around my face. The same smell inside the space suit with the round glass helmet that my head disappears into. My body comfortably hides in the hermetic cocoon with its big, soft paws—inside I move my hands, enjoying the slow movements. My thumbs, magnified ten times over, wiggle impossibly far away from me. I'm ready to go out into the open cosmos, or at least I'm technically ready.

The pre-launch program has been reduced to a minimum. Shatrov isn't happy about it, but what can you do? I suspect that he soothes his conscience at night with vodka. Poor guy—he probably has to buy the bottle with his own money, taken from his miserable salary. He even unscrews the cap, but only lets me sniff it—*Kosmicheskaya*, with three red stars skewered above a blue rocket, like a drawing out of a children's book.

I ought to buy him a few rounds, I say to myself, I should come up with some kind of present for him once everything's finished. Because, I assume that I'll see him again *at the end*. I haven't been completely informed regarding that question, but Shatrov has been with me continually since the very beginning, eighteen hours a day. It would seem impossible for him not to be the first one to greet me when the capsule with the landing apparatus hits the soft black earth, the wheat fields of Kazakhstan.

>>>

Traveling in space has many wonderful aspects and one terrible one—which is the further away you get from the earth, the more visible the distance between you and your earthly life becomes. And it becomes that much sadder and harder for you to accept the magnitude of the time needed to return. This feeling grows and keeps growing, except if you decide not to return at all.

But the most important thing is to scatter K-shev's ashes completely, with no leftovers, in the airless, non-orbital cosmos.

>>>

The rocket is beautiful, beautiful and proud. Where is Comrade Todorov, my morals and law teacher, if only he could see me now. Look, Comrade Todorov—and you thought I was joking. Do you see me?—that's me in one of the reclining seats in the cockpit surrounded by all these machines. Metal, uniformly spaced rivets. I don't know which one holds more significance for my life—Chernobyl or Baikonur? Perhaps both things had to happen to me, in precisely the right order. Because I now possess a body of cells that have been irradiated deep down. A body that sits calmly and decisively in the transport cabin. The cosmos calls to me. The very same cosmos promised by those reprinted Russian popular science books from my childhood. School bulletin boards and pictures from *Pioneers and Rockets* magazine, strangely mixing into the general brownish-blue mass. The rocket now is beautiful and majestic.

The rocket, *Energia*, a thousand-ton giant. The terror of seeing the enormous mechanism, which was created to start up only once. I see a square of its light hull through the cockpit's side window. The reusable space shuttle *Buran*—pride of the erstwhile Soviet space and aeronautical industry—attached to the launch rocket with three hydraulic and three mechanical suction cups. Tucked beneath them are the pyrotechnical systems, stuck on with a gray gum, the glue that guards against an undesirable premature explosion. Later, in orbit, this final stage will also become unnecessary. And then the soft explosions will pry them apart: the *Energia* from the *Buran* on its side, and the *Buran* from the *Energia*, until recently hitched together. They will reach that cherished altitude and afterward never meet again. Except perhaps in the ions of the glittering atmosphere, on its grating upper edges. There, where the corona of earthly air comes up against the cosmic nothingness. There, when the shuttle returns through the sizzling layers, breaking them like chains. In the flames washing over its hull, the *Buran* will again caress the slender rocket. The *Energy*, broken up, shattered into basic pieces, will once again embrace the shuttle.

In this vortex of ions, under the rasping of the file with which the universe crafts the galvanic globe of the stratosphere and sands away the calluses from the cosmos' feet as if with a galactic pumice stone—amid the physique of the cosmic bodies, nothing will remain of K-shev's body (nor even his ashes, I hope).

"And that's why, Comrade Todorov, astronautics hides more symbolism than can be seen on the surface of its realistic principles. That's why flying is so beautiful."

I hope that he understands me, finally.

>>>

The desire for freedom, that is at the root of everything. As long as there's a law, it doesn't matter what law, freedom does not yet truly exist. Lawlessness is the only absolutely free territory, there rules are created at every individual moment and only last that long.

In that sense I believe, Comrade Todorov, that the first of all natural laws best summarizes this tension: the law of gravity versus the freedom to overcome it.

Leaving, becoming distant from yourself, that's at the basis of weightlessness. When you break away from your earthly stance, when you leave your orbit as well, the planets shrink in the portholes. Your individual body becomes the center of all attraction. You spin in the vacuum-womb like a stellar baby, who is the beginning and end of everything, just as it is its very self.

But I am nevertheless the product of the pedagogical and educational system in which I was raised. For that reason, even at the moment when I can already imagine that *I myself* have turned out to be the great and supernatural Prime Mover, the omnipresent factor behind the Big Bang, the Great Attractor from physics textbooks—even then, I still keep thinking about him, worrying about K-shev. What more could he possibly want with us? Hasn't all his power over me been toppled, along with the repeal of the principle of the Party's supremacy?

Yes, that's how it seems at first glance. But after all the old norms have been obliterated and you have been left and are left

on your own—with the mechanism of pure causes and effects—
then the only working principle remaining comes to the forefront.
And that is the Law of the Right of the Firstcomer.

Today I judge him for things that he probably wouldn't do if
he could see them as I do—from the position of time. My accusations would be part of his conscience, if only everything could be
given a new order. If I could be *him*, or vice-versa—he could be
me. It looks very simple, a question of chronology in time. The
bodies with which and over which we battle—his, mine, hers—
are, in fact, the battlefield.

One critical, criminal question hangs over everything, however: Why am I rehashing all of this? Why, through her purifying
body, the body of K-shev's daughter, am I approaching the very
same place where her father also is—the narrow transitional space
of death? Could it be that the most horrifying part has already
begun, the part I have always feared exactly as much as growing
up? Has the process of *transforming into K-shev* begun?

Going Back

So for that reason I go back to earth, to his bedside, amid the
signals of reality. Outside a truck relieves the dumpsters of trash
with a steady hum.

In the end, I have to reach out—I take the envelope sitting on
the nightstand. There's a name written on it. Even in the cramped
letters of the sickly script I recognize that his hand has written it:

"*A letter to my son.*"

His Son

"*I wanted you to love me for what I am. For that reason I never pretended. Was that terrible? Now I'm dying, dying of a disease that I
almost brought on you, too. Forgive me.*"

Blah-blah, and so on. He's sleeping now and will probably never wake up again. So he must've fallen asleep for good, since he finally decided to write. He's fallen into those forms of the words "eternity" and "sleep" that are used in obituaries. Is there any point in reading any further? Why, for something new that I don't already know?

"Of course, first of all, that unnatural Article One had to be repealed. But a change in the law still doesn't mean a judgment. Once my leading and fatherly role has been rejected, you both can invite someone else into the vacant position. Anyone else. My end is near—I assume the two of you won't wait much longer. There's money in the briefcase. More than a million, I hope it'll be enough. I don't have any more, that's all of it. Don't be afraid, go ahead and take it, stow it away somewhere. I don't need painkillers anymore, the drugs are useless at this point.

I'm now looking at my hands. Believe me, I can't feel anything anymore. If someone comes close to me, even very close, I can't feel it. I touch the sheets, I can still move my fingers, but it's as if I'm not touching anything.

I'm on the bed, half-turned on my side—that's how they leave me during the day. For a long while now I've spent all my time lying down and hungry, because I can't swallow any food. They don't feed me, they just give me nutrients through the IV. But I'm still hungry, I'm hungry. They inject some chemical so I don't feel the hunger, so I won't want to eat—but I'm hungry, my stomach is empty. They say it's already gotten thinner, burned up or something with the intestines. I don't know what it is, but I feel hunger. My teeth are falling out, the holes are numb and empty, but I still want to chew. I'm hungry, come and feed me, or nurse me—with bare gums, toothless, I can suckle from your breasts. Can't you see how much I need you, my girl?"

"Filthy old man!" I feel like telling him. "You've got the wrong address. Shut up, you make me sick!"

117

Then: Shhh.

The shushing comes from behind my back.

"Shhhh, be quiet," she whispers and takes a step forward. Unbuttoning the buttons just above her breasts.

"Don't do it," I tell her, *don't*, I beg her.

"Shut up," she waves her hand, brushing me aside. "Leave, or if you want, stay. Watch, but be quiet."

I see her, I see him. He opens his mouth, I see it—his lips open thirstily.

>>>

The fusion that splits you into halves—yet a strange wholeness is somehow achieved along with it. Something made up of its own parts, but in a different configuration. This connection is preda-tory—*it* is the predator—and that is precisely what is so painful for her.

She wants to feel the supercharged particles—how they change the shape and contents of the cells with the invisible vibrations of their heavy neutrons. They shove aside the cell membranes, warp the mitochondria's soft form, and derail the nuclei from their orbits. She wanted—at least on the day of those May Day demonstrations, on the bright white day of Chernobyl—to change something. She sensed a great opportunity to correct the genes: not mine, not his, and if possible, not even her own anymore. And in this way she is not mine, not his. Free, finally.

"You want to run away," I hear K-shev say.

He is speaking both to me and to her, simultaneously. "You're striving toward this illness, I realize, as if toward salvation. I'd have let you go, you know, if it had been possible. But it wasn't."

"Why? Why?!" I scream voicelessly with my eyes, since she has forbidden me all sounds and words. I scream as they fuse together, and I know that she feels him in her stomach like a knife:

"Why?"

A simple answer, thus terrible and unnerving:

"Because I love you too much."

I don't know who is guilty, but I do know who's going to pay for all of this—the price was a question of time. Our horror ends in one and the same moment, spread out like a roll of thunder. Her flat, still childlike stomach. The wall against which my waves are doomed to break.

Check-out

I sit up in bed. I can reach out exactly far enough to grab the knife off the table. In my crazed hunger I had pounced on—and eaten (last night, I think it was last night)—devoured the food, and the knife remained there, like a harmful convenience—why?

Why am I cutting my ankle three or four times—three or four lines (I'd like even more)—but it's best to stop.

A stream of blood seeps through the leg of my jeans, and then another one next to it. Soon it isn't even beautiful anymore, just a shapeless red stripe. The splotches slowly soak through, I can feel how the threads in the cloth swell up, like the black crumbs on a slice of toast as they soften up from the butter—the butter, the blood saturates them. The night rolls back, the morning comes, the train of black hours gathers up its cars full of ghostly passengers. The world of nighttime fears is terrifying due to the emptiness that surrounds its characters. In the blackness, their dim faces don't cast back reflections. But the light—here it is again, the new, tolerable, daytime face of death. The death, so to speak, that appeals to us.

Come on, I say to myself, let's start thinking about bodily functions. The body is alive, so it's born to die. Death, considered realistically, shouldn't frighten us. My pant legs are heavy, the blood streams out.

So now she finally comes out of the bathroom, buttoning up her clothes. She looks around with a very strange gaze, the eyes of a person who hasn't found what she wanted. But if I were to ask her what she was really looking for, what more she could want from an empty hotel room—hotel rooms are always somehow empty, despite the furniture, despite the luggage—would she be able to formulate her desire? What does she know about me besides my name?

"So you're really his son, then?"

I open the briefcase and give her a pack of bills.

"So he's sick, huh? That sucks. Too bad."

I notice she's looking at the money, however, as she folds a piece of gum into her mouth and mashes it between her front teeth:

"I don't have a father. It's better that way."

She combs her hair in front of the mirror, puts on lipstick.

"So I don't have to worry about whether he's sick now, somewhere or with something."

She rubs her lips together, smearing the lipstick, fixing the edges with her finger.

"I don't even want to know his name."

The name *sick* passes within a hair's breadth of the concept *healthy*, I think to myself.

She opens the door, looks around the room—at the money, of course—then exhales and without saying goodbye, walks out.

What a strange coincidence, COMING ACROSS A BUL-GARIAN GIRL ON THE REEPERBAHN. I don't know, Hamburg really is a strange city.

I also don't know whether it is acceptable to bring prostitutes to this hotel, but it's a little late to ask.

The guys at reception look at me strangely, but don't say anything. The key drops into the marble box that says:

"Thank you! Please come visit us again."

I pay without saying a word and without staggering.

>>>

At dawn the rats are hopping lightly along the canal. I step aside onto the grass—the green, I think to myself, will soak up the blood. I shouldn't leave a trace on the clean pathway, I think to myself, on the blue asphalt—in my imagination it can now serve as a bridge, which finally leads to the beyond.

NOTES ON THE TRANSLATION

p. 26: Parody of the poem "Northern Lights" by the proletarian poet Hristo Smirnenski (1898-1923).

p. 47: Bulgarian cosmonauts participated in the Soviet space program. The first Bulgarian visited space in 1979 on the Russian ship *Soyuz-33*. The second—and for the time being, the final—Bulgarian cosmonaut blasted off in 1988, several years before the break up of the USSR.

p. 62: A line from the song "Unlived Things" (1985) by The Crickets, the most popular Bulgarian rock group of its day, formed in 1967.

p. 63: This is a line from another Crickets' song, "I Am Simply a Person" (1990).

p. 71: Anton Semenovych Makarenko was a pre-World War II Soviet pedagogue who created an educational system for homeless children living in colonies in Russia. To Bulgarian schoolchildren, this system was a symbol of harsh order and cruel discipline.

p. 97: A parody of the song "As I'm Loving You" by the Argirovi Brothers, a Bulgarian pop duo made up of the identical twins Blagovest and Svetoslav. They were among the most popular stars during the 1980s and the perestroika era.

p. 98: A mausoleum stood in the center of the Bulgarian capital from 1949 to 1999, housing the mummified body of Georgi Dimitrov, the leader of the Bulgarian Communist Party and the general secretary of Comintern.

p. 109: A parody of the poem "Bulgaria" by Communist poet Georgi Dzhagarov (1925-1995).

p. 110: A line from the song "At Every Kilometer" (1969), the theme music from the Socialist-era propagandistic television series of the same name, which was the most widely viewed program in Bulgaria during the 20th century.

p. 117: A play on the Bulgarian word *chlen*, which can mean both "the male sex organ" and "a legal article," as in the notorious Article One of Bulgaria's socialist constitution: "The People's Republic of Bulgaria is a socialist state, headed by the urban and rural Working Class. The leading power in society and the state is the Bulgarian Communist Party. The Bulgarian Communist Party leads the founding of a mature socialist society" (1971).

Georgi Tenev, before penning the Vick Prize-winning novel *Party Headquarters*, had already published four books, founded the Triumviratus Art Group, hosted *The Library* television program about books, and written plays that have been performed in Germany, France, and Russia. He is also a screenwriter for film and TV.

Angela Rodel earned an MA in linguistics from UCLA and received a Fulbright Fellowship to study Bulgarian. In 2010, she won a PEN Translation Fund Grant for Georgi Tenev's short story collection. She is one of the most prolific translators of Bulgarian literature working today.

Open Letter—the University of Rochester's nonprofit, literary translation press—is one of only a handful of publishing houses dedicated to increasing access to world literature for English readers. Publishing ten titles in translation each year, Open Letter searches for works that are extraordinary and influential, works that we hope will become the classics of tomorrow.

Making world literature available in English is crucial to opening our cultural borders, and its availability plays a vital role in maintaining a healthy and vibrant book culture. Open Letter strives to cultivate an audience for these works by helping readers discover imaginative, stunning works of fiction and poetry, and by creating a constellation of international writing that is engaging, stimulating, and enduring.

Current and forthcoming titles from Open Letter include works from Argentina, Catalonia, China, Iceland, Israel, Latvia, Poland, Spain, South Africa, and many other countries.

www.openletterbooks.org